MASQUERADE

MASQUERADE

SHERI WHITEFEATHER

HEAT
New York

THE BERKLEY PUBLISHING GROUP
Published by the Penguin Group
Penguin Group (USA) Inc.
375 Hudson Street, New York, New York 10014, USA
Penguin Group (Canada), 90 Eglinton Avenue East, Suite 700, Toronto, Ontario M4P 2Y3, Canada
(a division of Pearson Penguin Canada Inc.)
Penguin Books Ltd., 80 Strand, London WC2R 0RL, England
Penguin Group Ireland, 25 St. Stephen's Green, Dublin 2, Ireland (a division of Penguin Books Ltd.)
Penguin Group (Australia), 250 Camberwell Road, Camberwell, Victoria 3124, Australia
(a division of Pearson Australia Group Pty. Ltd.)
Penguin Books India Pvt. Ltd., 11 Community Centre, Panchsheel Park, New Delhi—110 017, India
Penguin Group (NZ), 67 Apollo Drive, Rosedale, North Shore 0632, New Zealand
(a division of Pearson New Zealand Ltd.)
Penguin Books (South Africa) (Pty.) Ltd., 24 Sturdee Avenue, Rosebank, Johannesburg 2196,
South Africa

Penguin Books Ltd., Registered Offices: 80 Strand, London WC2R 0RL, England

This book is an original publication of The Berkley Publishing Group.

This is a work of fiction. Names, characters, places, and incidents either are the product of the author's imagination or are used fictitiously, and any resemblance to actual persons, living or dead, business establishments, events, or locales is entirely coincidental. The publisher does not have any control over and does not assume any responsibility for author or third-party websites or their content.

PRINTING HISTORY
Heat trade paperback edition / April 2010

Library of Congress Cataloging-in-Publication Data

Whitefeather, Sheri.
  Masquerade / Sheri Whitefeather.—Heat trade pbk. ed.
    p. cm.
  ISBN 978-0-425-23243-9 (trade pbk.)
  1. Triangles (Interpersonal relations)—Fiction. I. Title.
PS3623.H5798M37 2010
813'.6—dc22   2009043810

PRINTED IN THE UNITED STATES OF AMERICA

10 9 8 7 6 5 4 3 2 1

MASQUERADE

PROLOGUE

A SMALL SEASIDE COUNTRY
EARLY TWENTIETH CENTURY

I knew better than to make eye contact with the stranger who'd caught my attention from across the ballroom. So I stood off to the side in my luxurious gown, stealing lash-lowered glances and praying that no one would notice. I was, after all, betrothed to the duke who owned this grand estate, and the curious stranger was my fiancé's guest.

Surely he was American. He was far too rugged to hail from Glenmoor or anywhere in Western Europe for that matter. Even attired in formalwear, he had an untamed quality. He stood tall and powerfully built, yet he seemed wiry, too, a sure-footed man who could move swiftly, who wasn't labored by his stature. His longish hair, dark brown in color, had been combed straight back, but a portion of it rebelled, falling across his forehead. I assumed the sun had bronzed his skin. But it was possible that he'd been born with a swarthy complexion, roughly enhanced by the elements. Tiny lines crinkled around deeply set eyes, and when he laughed at something another guest said, he tossed back his head in a strong, confident manner. I imagined him as the hero of a Beadle's Dime Novel, much like the wildly compelling stories I'd read about Jesse James.

America fascinated me so.

By now, a small grouping of men had gathered around the stranger. He was infectious, and not just to me. I wanted to join them, but it wouldn't be decorous for me to do so. Sometimes I detested being female. And a titled one, no less.

Lady Ellen Fairmont. Yes, that was me. At twenty-two, I was fair and blonde and gently curved—the socially refined, properly reared daughter of a womanizing earl who'd gambled away the family fortune. To cover his debts, Papa had arranged a marriage for me. Mama agreed that it was for the best. But why wouldn't she? Papa had lost our home in a card game. Currently, we all lived here, with my parents acting as my chaperones. After the wedding, they would be awarded a small estate of their own.

My betrothed was a good man. None came finer. Stuart Harris, Duke of Auburn, possessed a heart as vast as his pocketbook.

Then why was I stealing glances at the stranger?

Shame coiled low in my belly. Truly, I should turn away and not look at him. But he was like a lighthouse beacon drawing me across an ocean mist. He made me feel warm and dreamy. Carnal, I thought, my shame deepening.

"Oh, my," said a woman, standing nearby.

I snapped to attention and shifted in the direction of her voice. Had she noticed me admiring the stranger?

Luckily, she hadn't. It was Lady Milford, a stunning brunette in her middle thirties, and she was too busy gauging him for herself. But she had the right, I suppose. She was widowed. Lord Milford had died a few years back, and it was rumored that she fancied free-spirited lovers to keep the boredom at bay.

"Who is that man?" she asked me.

"What man?" I responded, feigning innocence.

"The tall, dark one." She tapped a gauntlet-gloved hand to her chin. "He looks wild, doesn't he? Like an outlaw."

My favorite dime store novels came to mind. "I hadn't noticed."

"So, you don't know who he is?"

"No, I'm sorry. I don't."

Just then, my fiancé approached. He was as tall as the

stranger, but that was where the similarity ceased. The duke's gray-threaded hair was impeccably styled, as was everything about him. He'd been born and bred for the life he led. At fifty-four, he was accustomed to wealth and privilege, to behaving in a manner that complemented his title.

If he had a sense of adventure, I'd yet to see it.

I would be his second wife. His first, a woman he'd dearly loved, had died of an illness, leaving him without an heir. All the tender years they'd shared had proved fruitless, and now the duke was hoping that our upcoming union would produce the heir she'd been unable to give him.

If only he wasn't so kind. There were times when I wanted to hate him, to fault him for the deal he'd struck with my father. Yet I knew I could have done worse.

"My lady," *he said, then indicated the direction of the stranger.* "I would like to introduce you to someone."

Beneath my lace-trimmed, pearl-encrusted gown, my guilty heart knocked against my corset. Still, I nodded dutifully. Of course, when didn't I? Dutiful was the word that best described me.

"Your Grace?" *Not to be ignored, Lady Milford addressed the duke.* "May I be introduced, too?"

If her bold request offended him, he didn't let it show. Forever the gentleman, he responded, "Most certainly," *and escorted both of us toward the stranger.*

Who, at that very moment, looked up and caught sight of us, too. As a smile skirted past his lips, he made direct eye contact with me. Swift as it was, I understood the secret he was trying to convey.

No one had noticed me watching him earlier. But he had.

He knew all along that I'd misbehaved.

CHAPTER ONE

Amber Pontiero enjoyed misbehaving. She lived to be bad. But as she stood at the front door of a Hollywood Hills rental house, she asked herself what the hell she was doing.

She had no business getting involved with two men. Sure, she'd already had a threesome with them last summer, but that was just a one-night fling. *This*, she told herself, as she prepared to ring the bell, could lead to something dangerous.

Something emotional. Something completely out of Amber's realm. Why? Because ever since the threesome, she couldn't get either of them out of her mind.

She glanced back at the street. The airport limo was still there, the driver waiting until she was admitted into the house. She wasn't scheduled to be here, at least not at this hour. She'd taken an earlier flight.

But in spite of arriving early, this visit wasn't a surprise. Jay and Luke, her former one-night flings, were expecting her. They'd all agreed that she would stay for a month.

Still poised to ring the bell, she looked down at her luggage. She hadn't brought a ton of luggage, but she didn't need to. Amber preferred to shop when she was on holiday, to buy whatever she needed in whatever city she was visiting.

As a rich and spoiled fashion heiress, she'd been everywhere and done just about everything. Her family had mansions all over the globe, including a beach house in Malibu. It wasn't as if Southern California was foreign to her. This was one of her playgrounds.

Naturally, she had the looks to go with her jet-setting lifestyle. She even spoke with a slightly European accent from all the years she'd spent in exclusive boarding schools. At twenty-seven, Amber was one cosmopolitan chick.

So why was she standing here with her pulse thudding in her throat?

Before the limo driver declared her insane, she rang the dang bell.

Footsteps sounded on the other side, and her heart thudded again. She took a quick moment to run a hand through her hair. Cut in an angular bob, it was dark and straight and shiny—retro Sassoon.

Her embossed tank top, pin-striped vest and short slim skirt had come from her mother's latest collection. Beneath her Pontiero couture, she was tan all over. Amber frequented clothes-optional beaches and sunbathed in the nude.

She waited a second longer, then boom!—the door flung open and there stood Jay Novak: actor, model, surfer, snowboarder, all around California guy. He wore his light brown hair short and just a little messy. Tall and leanly muscled, he sported a tee shirt and Hawaiian-print shorts.

A grin stretched across his handsome face, and she realized that although they'd done all sorts of decadent things to each other, she barely knew him.

Same with Luke, her other partner in sex. She'd met both men through their talent agencies, but she'd hooked up with them at a masquerade ball. Amber's mother had been hosting the ball at her Santa Fe, New Mexico, mansion, and Jay and Luke had been hired to impersonate another guest.

In the costumes, makeup and wigs that had been provided, Jay, Luke and the other guest had looked remarkably similar. In real life, they resembled each other, too. But not to the point of mixing them up, not like at the ball.

The other guest was a former lover of Amber's, and he'd been playing a trick on his new lover to see if she could tell him apart from the other two men. Amber had helped arrange the charade, suggesting that each man wear a different-colored rose on his lapel, which had become their identities that night.

Luckily the tricked lover had picked the right man. Caught up in the fun, Amber had zeroed in on the other two, flirting shamelessly and then inviting them to her room.

During the threesome they'd turned out the lights and the men had kept on their masks, heightening the thrill and making it difficult for her to distinguish between them.

Since the masquerade, Jay and Luke had become friends and roommates, making her wonder if they'd been sharing other women the way they'd shared her. Both of them were highly heterosexual though. Amber didn't dally with bisexual men. She preferred having the male attention all for herself, which she'd gotten that night.

Regardless, she hoped they weren't having other ménages. She wanted their threesome to be exclusive. Special, she supposed, which was downright stupid.

"You're here," Jay said, shattering the stare-at-each-other silence. "And you're gorgeous as ever."

"You, too."

He came forward to hug her, and she got a sexy chill. She deliberately bumped his cock and felt him shudder. He turned to kiss her, and their mouths came together in illicit remembrance.

Lord, he was hot. She could've mauled him forever. Every detail, every hot, naughty image of their night together zinged through her body.

Only something was missing.

No, not something. Someone.

She ended the connection, took a deep breath and asked, "Where's Luke?" She wanted a tongue-thrusting kiss from him, too.

"He had an audition today. He'll be back in a while." Jay paused. "One man isn't enough for you?"

Did she detect a note of jealousy?

"Sometimes. But I prefer multiple partners." Because the more lovers she had, the less of a commitment she had to make. "Ménages are my favorite."

He picked up her bags, inviting her into the house. "Then I'm glad I can oblige. Our threesome was the wildest night of my life."

"Mine, too." And that was saying a lot. The reason, she assumed, why she craved this reunion and was spending the next month with him and Luke.

Jay smiled and the note of jealousy was gone. Or maybe she'd imagined it. From what she recalled, he seemed to be the less possessive of the two. Less romantic, too. Luke, she decided, was the one to watch out for. The day after the masquerade, she'd received two long-stemmed roses. One had been pink, the other red, representing the boutonnieres the men had worn on their costumes the night before. Soon after, she discovered the roses had been Luke's idea and Jay had simply gone along with it.

Amber preferred to downplay romantic gestures. But even so, she'd fussed over the flowers, drying the loose petals and placing them in an antique powder compact for safekeeping.

She glanced back at the limo and waved the driver on his way. As the car pulled away from the curb, she prayed that she wasn't getting in over her head.

Men weren't supposed to have this kind of effect on her. Single, double or otherwise.

She checked out Jay's butt on the way inside. He and his roommate were exactly the same height, with the same physique.

"This is it," Jay said.

She realized he was talking about the house. By now, they were in the living room. "It's really nice." She assumed it had been built in the late 1920s or early 1930s from the art deco style. She noticed the fireplace had a geometric motif. The art deco theme continued with a red leather sofa, a matching armchair and black lacquer tables. She took a second glance around. "It's so tidy." Everything seemed to be in its place.

He laughed. "We cleaned up when we knew you were coming. It doesn't always look like this."

"Thanks for thinking of me."

"Sure. But it'll probably be a mess before long."

"Whose furniture is it?"

"Luke's. I think he got it at a flea market or something."

"Good finds." Amber was used to the best of everything, but she appreciated artistic ingenuity.

"Yeah, I guess so. He's lived here for a while. He had another roommate. But when the other guy quit paying his share of the rent, Luke kicked him out and asked me if I wanted to room with him."

Which, she concluded, was ideal for her . . . having them under the same roof. She walked over to the glass doors that led to the backyard and peered out. "There's a pool?"

"A hot tub, too. No way was I going to turn this place down." He came to stand beside her. "It rocks."

"It does." She liked the Old Hollywoodness of it. When they opened the door and walked outside, she admired the view.

"I'm glad you're here," he said.

"Me, too." She turned to face him, and he zeroed in for another kiss, pulling her closer and making her pussy clench.

"We can go skinny-dipping," he whispered against her lips. "The three of us."

She wanted to slide her hands down his shorts and fondle his rising erection, but she refrained. It wouldn't be the same without Luke. "I like how you think."

"You came here for a ménage, and that's what I'm going to give you."

"Luke, too?"

"Does he have a choice?"

"No. But is it what he wants?"

"He's got a major thing for you, Amber. And if it means having me there, too, he'll deal with it."

Not too major, she hoped. She was already struggling with her own rose-petals attachment. "He's anxious to be with me again?"

"He's half insane over it."

So was she, but she kept that thought to herself. Instead, she asked what had been on her mind earlier. "Have you two been sharing other women?"

"Not even close. It only happened because of you."

Meaning what? That they never would've ended up in the same bed with the same woman if she hadn't seduced them that night? Did that mean they were both more monogamous than she was?

Did it matter? She was only going to party with them for the next month. After that, she would leave their affair behind.

"Where am I going to sleep?" she asked.

"Luke wanted you to stay in his room, and I wanted you in mine, so we decided to set up the guest room for the three of us instead."

She smiled. "Your idea, no doubt?"

He smiled back. "I'm the peacekeeper."

And the less possessive one, she reminded herself. She reached up to skim his classic-cut jaw. "I like you."

"I like you, too." He flashed his signature grin—the laid-back California guy. "Wanna fuck me before Luke gets home? That would make him crazy, especially if he walked in on us."

She arched her brows. Already the competition was starting, with her as the prize. "Crazy jealous? Or crazy horny?"

He pondered her question, then said, "Probably both."

"Nice try, but I'll wait until I can have both of you together."

He held up three fingers. "I know. Ménage à trois." He said the last part with an exaggerated French accent.

She rolled her eyes and laughed. It was tempting to take him up on his offer, but somehow she couldn't do that to Luke.

Was that her way of being monogamous? She glanced at the kidney-shaped pool and attached Jacuzzi. No, she thought. That was just her way of sticking to the two-boys/one-girl plan.

"Will you show me the guest room?" she asked, curious to see their quarters.

"Sure."

They returned to the house and walked down the hall, with him carrying her bags. She passed their rooms with barely a peek at either. Later, she would explore how each of them lived within his own masculine space.

The guest room did a number on her. The first thing she noticed was the big exquisite vase of pink and red roses on the dresser. Damn, she thought. Luke had done it again.

"His idea?" she asked, although she already knew the answer.

"Twenty-nine flowers. One for each day that you're going to be here."

"He counted the days?"

"He's weird that way." Not to be outdone, Jay added, "I have a surprise for you, too."

Intrigued, she batted her lashes, teasing him the way he'd teased her with the phony French accent. "For *moi*? What is it?"

"I'm going to cook for you. I'm going to be the chef around here."

"You have culinary skills?" Somehow he didn't seem the type.

"I work part-time as a fusion-style cook. But, hey, I'm an actor. I've run the gamut of restaurant work."

"Then by all means, cook away. I adore being waited on."

"Yeah, that's what I figured. Pampered heiress that you

are." He shifted his weight, as if something were shifting in his mind.

"What?" she asked.

"Nothing."

"Come on, Jay. You're thinking about something." Something that mattered to him. She might be rich and spoiled, but she knew there was more to the world than her privileged corner of it.

"It's just that I haven't cooked for a woman since . . ."

"Since what?"

"My divorce."

"You were married?" Maybe he was more possessive than she'd given him credit for.

"Yes, but it didn't last very long, less than a year."

Regardless, she got the troubling sense that he hadn't gotten over his ex. "Do want to talk about it?"

"Not particularly." He sat down on the bed. "What about you? Any marriages in your broom closet?"

Amber took a quick breath. "Me? No way." When she was younger, she'd wanted desperately to be a bride. She'd planned every aspect of her wedding, with whatever father had been available to walk her down the aisle. But she'd stopped believing in the sanctity of marriage after her fourth—yes, fourth—father had turned out to be as worthless as the other three.

Was it any wonder she preferred to control her affairs? To remain uncommitted?

She sat next to Jay, letting him protect his past while she protected hers.

Before too much time ticked by, she started a new conversation. "This is a nice big bed. A California king?"

"It was another of Luke's ideas."

"Because it has enough room to keep you on your own side of it."

"Yeah, but with you in the middle." He scanned the length of her. "So when are we going to do this?"

She feigned innocence. "Do what?"

"The resurrected threesome. Can we do it as soon as Luke gets home or are you going to make us wait?"

"I haven't decided."

"Tease."

She smiled, and stood up, enjoying his perusal. Making the most of it, she began to unpack, allowing him to watch her walk about the room.

Because the bed took up so much room, the furniture was sparse. Still, the room was nicely decorated. The antique satinwood dresser that held the flowers needed a bit of restoration, but it appealed to her. So did the vanity table. She assumed the items had been purchased specifically for her visit, probably by Luke.

As she arranged her lingerie in a drawer, Jay said, "Do you have any idea how beautiful you really are?"

Amber had been praised for her appearance her entire life. But hearing him say it made her feel wildly desirable. She turned to look at him, and their gazes locked.

He blew out the breath in his lungs. "I don't want to wait. This is torture."

"That's what women do. Torture men. It's part of our job."

"No kidding."

Was his remark directed solely at her or did his ex have something to do with it? Amber knew better than to care, but his expression made her curious. He seemed trapped between hunger and despair. Maybe she should just go ahead and fuck him. It would certainly make him feel better.

But she couldn't bring herself to do it, not without Luke being part of the mix.

A blowjob then? She glanced at the front of his shorts. He was already half-aroused, and she remembered how big he got when he was in full-fellatio mode.

As big as Luke, she thought.

On the masquerade night, she'd given both of them head, back and forth, one right after the other. Since they'd both been masked at the time with lights off, it had been one of the naughtiest, most erotic acts she'd ever performed. Who was who hadn't mattered.

Still didn't, she told herself.

She was only in it for the fun. Jay's personal life shouldn't concern her, nor should Luke's romantic nature.

Then why did she want to ask Jay about his ex? And why did the flowers on the dresser make her even more anxious to see Luke?

Those damn childhood dreams, that's why. The bridal bullshit, she thought, struggling to clear her mind.

"Why don't you fix me a snack?" she said.

He frowned a little. "Right now?"

"Yes, right now. You're supposed to pamper me."

He managed a grin. The casual California guy was back. "How about something that involves whipped cream?"

Score one for the boy, she thought. "We'll do whipped cream another time." The three of them, she added mentally. "I'm more in the mood for something healthy."

"Raw veggies and low-fat artichoke dip?"

"Yes, that's perfect."

"It'll take me about twenty minutes to cook the dip. It's supposed to be served hot."

"Hot works for me."

"Yeah, I know." Another grin. "Hot is your middle name."

"Actually, it's Noelle. I was born near Christmas."

"Really?" He seemed surprised that she'd revealed a non-sexual piece of herself.

She was surprised, too. Now she wanted to take it back. Amber Noelle Pontiero preferred to remain on a femme fatale level.

Jay clasped her hand and led her to the kitchen, which had an art deco vibe, too, boasting a vintage enamel-topped table. Obviously, it belonged to Luke. So what was the deal with Jay? Had he gone minimalist after his divorce, not caring if he owned much of anything?

"Where did you live before you moved in here?" she asked.

"In an apartment in Burbank." He went to the fridge and removed a container of low-fat plain yogurt, low-fat mayonnaise, parmesan cheese and an onion.

"By yourself?"

"Yep."

"For how long?"

"About two years."

"Where's all of your stuff?"

"In my room. My apartment was a single."

Amber nodded, more to herself than to him. That explained his lifestyle after the divorce. Was two years a long time to be alone? She didn't know. She always surrounded herself with people. She decided that it was good for Jay to be here with her and Luke. That he needed the threesome as much as she did.

After preheating the oven, he retrieved a can of artichokes from the cabinet and opened it with a manual can opener, even though there was an electric model on the counter. Once he drained the can, he went about chopping the artichokes into bite-size pieces. He diced about a quarter of the onion, too.

While Amber stood nearby in her short skirt and high-heeled sandals, he combined the ingredients and seasoned the entire mixture with crushed red pepper.

From there, Jay transferred the mixture into a casserole dish and popped it in the oven.

When he went about cleaning and cutting raw vegetables, she considered how incredibly handsome he was and how intriguing it was to watch him work. She loved the idea of having a man cook for her.

She sat at the kitchen table and angled her body toward him. She was tempted to do a *Basic Instinct*, but she crossed her legs in ladylike fashion. Besides, Sharon Stone hadn't been wearing panties. Amber wore Chantilly lace from La Perla. "Can you make veal scallopini?"

"Why? Is that your favorite meal?"

"It's one of them."

"Then I'll learn to make it."

Good answer, she thought, wondering if his ex used to ravish him in the kitchen, if that was part of why he liked to cook.

Twenty minutes later, the snack was done. He sat down at the table with her, and they shared the hot, flavorful dip.

"Guilt-free food," she said, licking it from a carrot stick.

He stared at her mouth. "Is that how you try to live your life? Guilt-free?"

"Is there any other way? I like being a party girl." She liked being the first one to walk away when it was over. Courtesy of her past, she supposed, of wasting her youth pining after her missing fathers.

Jay took the carrot she'd been licking and ate it. "How about some champagne to go with it?"

"Why not?" She was always up for a little bubbly.

"It's the cheap stuff."

"That's okay." Sometimes she wore trashy clothes for the fun of it, so why not indulge in cheap champagne?

He went to the fridge, popped the cork on a low-budget bottle and filled two equally inexpensive flutes. After rejoining her at the table, they toasted their upcoming union.

She smiled, anticipating the ménage. "To the three of us."

Just then, the front door rattled, and Amber's heartbeat quickened.

Luke, the man who would complete their lust-driven trio, was home.

CHAPTER TWO

Amber stayed at the table, as did Jay.

"Hey, dude," Jay called out to his roommate. "I'm in the kitchen."

"I'm going to change," the other man replied.

When Luke bypassed the kitchen and headed for his room, Amber raised her eyebrows at Jay. "You didn't tell him I was here." Luke wouldn't be expecting her at this hour. Her original flight wouldn't have landed yet.

"You surprised me. Let him be surprised, too."

She nodded, then sipped the bubbly, not wanting Jay to know how anxious she was.

Luke didn't stay in his room for long. Soon he reentered the hallway, and from the sound of his footsteps, he appeared to be heading toward the guest room. Was he checking on their shared accommodations, making sure everything was just so?

Jay grinned. "He's going to know you're here now."

Yes, of course. Between her partially unpacked luggage and the lingerie drawer she'd left open, her whereabouts were clear. "Do you have to look so amused?"

"Why shouldn't I? He's not going to like that I got to see you first."

Here we go, she thought, with a tad of annoyance. The competition. She'd come here to share herself with them, not have them battle over her.

Jay started counting backwards from ten, like a New Year's celebration.

"Eight . . . seven . . . six . . . five . . ."

Stomp. Stomp.

In walked Luke, all tall and dark and riddled with angst. He looked at Amber, and her breath caught deep in her throat. But not audibly. She wouldn't dare make a vulnerable sound.

With the grace of a professional playgirl, she got up, walked toward him and flashed a siren's smile. Luke didn't return the smile. He remained intense.

She could tell that he wanted to kiss her senseless, but he didn't want Jay there when he did it.

Not good, she thought. Not for a threesome.

"Don't just stand there," Jay said to his roommate. "Go ahead and kiss her. I already did," he added, rubbing a bit of salt into the competitive wound.

"Don't tell me what to do," Luke replied, behaving like the warrior he was.

He was a mixed-blood Native American from the Mississippi band of Choctaw, and he spoke with a slight drawl, a voice that gave Amber erotic goose bumps.

She didn't know what he'd been wearing before, but he'd changed into a pair of washed-out jeans and a casual button-down shirt. His medium-length hair, dark and thick and straight, had been styled to frame his face. With naturally tanned skin and sharp-cut features, he was much more exotic-looking than Jay, but somehow they still resembled each other.

She wondered if they would be willing to do another masquerade. Goodness, she hoped so. She wanted to have fun with their monthlong ménages.

Finally, Luke took what he wanted. He reached out and grabbed her, so tightly he nearly knocked the air out of her lungs. When he dropped his hands and clutched her ass, dragging her pelvis against his, she teetered on her heels. In the process, he unwittingly hiked up the back of her skirt.

Talk about a naughty-girl moment. For Amber, it was the best kind of foreplay, especially since Luke didn't realize that he was giving Jay an unobstructed view of her La Perla–clad derriere.

When Luke kissed her, it was as hard and powerful as the ridge beneath his jeans.

As his tongue swept her mouth, she unbuttoned the front of his shirt and bared a portion of his chest.

Still seated, Jay went restless. He left the table and came closer. Suddenly, she could feel him behind her. Every nerve ending pulsed, especially those between her legs.

Sensing his roommate's proximity, Luke ended the kiss.

Then silence. Complete silence.

"She wants both of us," Jay reminded Luke.

"I know" came the harsh reply.

"If you know, then why are you resisting?"

"I'm not," Luke argued. "But one of these times, I want her all to myself."

"Those are the breaks, bro."

"I'm not your brother."

"You look like you could be." Jay pushed Luke's hands off of her ass and claimed that region for himself. "And that's part of why she wants us."

Sandwiched between two aggressive men, Amber listened to them talk about her as if she weren't there. Only they knew damn well she was. By now, their hard-ons were pressed against her, one in front and one in the rear.

Luke cursed and kissed her, picking up where he'd left off. Jay kissed her, too, nibbling roughly on the back of her neck. They weren't playing nice, but they were still playing.

When Luke came up for air, he spoke quietly. "Promise you'll be alone with me sometime."

Amber didn't respond. His piercing gaze arrowed straight through her.

"Promise," he insisted.

Jay caught wind of the conversation and joined in.

"Answer him," he told her.

Damn it, she thought. Pressure from both sides. Now they were doubling up on her. But wasn't that the reason she was here? For a game of dirty doubles?

Exactly, she told herself. One-on-one sex wasn't part of the arrangement, and she wouldn't let them bully her into it.

"No," she told Luke. "No time alone."

His reaction? He stepped away from her, but his gaze remained dark and piercing.

The distance he'd created left her feeling oddly empty, but she had too much pride to let it show.

Jay defended his roommate and stepped away from her, too. So there she was, without either of them.

"Screw you guys," she said.

Behind her, Jay chuckled. "Good luck with that."

Not used to being rejected, she spun around to glare at him. "At first you were competing with Luke, and now you're defending him and going all bromance? You two don't know what you want."

"We want you," Luke said, from the other side.

She turned again, facing the intense one. The warrior. The man who wanted a promise she wasn't willing to give. "You can have me, as long as you share. No separate playtime."

"Why not? What's the big deal?"

The deal was that she preferred to think of them as two halves that made a whole. "I want to re-create what we had before."

"Yeah, but Jay and I aren't conjoined twins. There are times we're going to need our space."

"It's only a month," she argued.

Luke stood his ground. "Just say yes."

"Come on, say yes," Jay parroted.

She moved to a spot where she could see both of them, rather than standing in the middle. She didn't want to be sandwiched between them, not unless it was during a sensual moment, and this wasn't her idea of erotic.

Still, the raw expression on Luke's face made her ache. She glanced at Jay, and he pulled off a smile. But that wasn't any better. His smile was almost as raw as Luke's expression. She imagined him smiling at his ex-wife that way when she was walking out the door.

She kept looking at Jay. "Do you want time alone with me, too?"

He nodded. "Probably as much as he does."

And probably for a completely different reason, she thought. The men looked alike, but they weren't alike.

What had she done? Coming here? Getting everyone's emotions tangled up?

She knew she should leave. But she couldn't seem to bring herself to do it.

"Okay," she said, hoping she was making the right decision. "I'll be with each of you alone, but not until after we play together, in all sorts of ways."

"Sounds good to me." This from Jay. But he was the more agreeable one.

Amber turned to Luke. "And you?"

He, of course, ended up challenging her. Rather than respond, he gave a tight nod.

Confused, she sighed. Hadn't he just gotten what he wanted? Or was he still uncertain about sharing her?

"You frustrate him," Jay said, by way of explanation.

She heaved another sigh. "So I gathered."

"It's because he's already half in love with you."

Oh, God, Amber thought. That wasn't funny. But Jay hadn't said it to be funny. He seemed quite serious.

"That isn't true," Luke snapped. "It isn't the least bit true."

She struggled to breathe. "Good. Fine. Now can we drop it?"

"Sure. Totally. It's dropped." He glanced over at Jay and mouthed a silent, "Fuck you."

The other man shrugged, then grinned. Nothing seemed to rattle him, except maybe his ex. But Amber was only guessing about that, assuming what the woman he'd married had meant to him.

"You better get this party started," Jay said to his roommate. "Or I will."

"Like hell." The loveless warrior scooped her into his arms. Just like that, he went caveman, carrying her down the hall. He paused at his own bedroom, and she suspected that he was tempted to break the rules and have her all to himself.

At this point, she might've let him. She felt ridiculously sexy in his arms. But then she glanced back and saw that Jay was following them, and he made her feel just as sexy. When he smiled, she got warm and wet between her legs. She hoped that she never had to choose between them.

Luke hauled her into the guest room and tossed her on the bed. Jay came forward and removed her shoes, and she realized they were going to undress her.

Luke went after her vest and tank top. Jay tugged at her skirt, and soon she was in her bra and panties.

They both told her how perfect she was, and she was glad that she'd seduced them at the ball.

Luke unhooked her bra, and Jay removed her panties, slowly, carefully.

Once she was bare, she lifted her hips, giving them a pretty view. Amber was smooth, completely waxed.

Luke leaned over to kiss her, taking her mouth by storm. He was an incredible kisser, and she slipped her arms around his neck to bring him closer.

Jay kissed her, too. Only he made his sweet foray along her inner thigh.

Glory.

Finally they were playing nice.

Luke's tongue swept in and out of her mouth, mimicking a lover's dance. He kneaded her breasts, making her nipples bead beneath his touch.

Then Jay, oh, Jay . . .

He found his way to her center and parted her slick folds. Dizzy, she moaned into Luke's mouth.

This was why she enjoyed ménages. This was the kind of intimacy she craved.

As Jay teased her clit, she moaned again. Luke stopped kissing her, and they gazed into each other's eyes.

"Do you like what he's doing to you?" he asked.

"Yes." She ran her fingertips along Luke's jaw, admiring

the handsome angles of his face. "It feels so good." So hot and wet.

"Are you going to come on him while you're staying close to me?"

"Yes," she said again. She liked the way he manipulated the foreplay. Although he was being possessive, he was still sharing her with his roommate.

For now, the threesome was all about Amber and her needs. Neither man had removed his clothing. Other than Luke's shirt being unbuttoned, they remained fully dressed.

She glanced down at Jay. Did he like the taste of her? The feminine flavor? Of course he did, she thought. He was a very sexual man. They both were.

Equal lovers. Equal balance.

She opened her legs a little wider. She tightened her rear a tad, too, scooting closer to Jay.

He accepted the invitation and slid his tongue all the way inside, lapping at her juices.

But it wasn't enough, and both men seemed to know exactly what she needed. Jay rolled over and Luke lifted her onto the other man's face.

Yes, Amber thought. Oh, yes.

She felt even more desirable this way, especially when Luke knelt behind her and pressed his body against hers. In a sense, he was straddling Jay, too. But it was the only way for him to stay close to Amber. Grasping her hips, he helped her rock back and forth.

Between the two of them, she was luckiest girl in Hollywood. No, in the world, she thought. It didn't get any more self-indulgent than this. They were letting her spoil herself.

Not that they wouldn't expect their turns. Eventually they would want their cocks sucked, and they would expect her to get down on her knees and do it right.

The thought excited her, and she wiggled against Jay's mouth.

"Are you being a bad girl in your mind?" Luke asked.

Impressed, she angled her shoulders, putting her face next to his. "How did you know?"

"I know everything about you, Amber. What you like. How you think. What gets you off."

"You can't know *everything*."

He slid his hands between her legs and opened her up nice and wide. "I can try."

Dually impressed, she realized that he was making Jay lick between his fingers in order to get to her.

"Now who's being bad?"

"I am," Luke responded. "But I'm doing it for you."

And Jay seemed to be doing it for all of them, enjoying the experience for what it was.

Captivated by his easy manner, she wondered what type

of woman he'd married. Innocent? Wild? Somewhere in between?

Luke nipped her earlobe, and she forgot about Jay's ex. But not completely. It made her wonder if Luke had an ex-wife. He actually seemed more like the marrying kind.

"Kiss me," he whispered.

She met his lips willingly and the connection was soft and sensual. She hoped that he'd never been anyone's husband. She liked having him all to herself.

A moment later, she changed the dangerous direction of her thoughts. She knew better than to care too deeply for either of them.

To prove that she was immune, she pulled away from Luke. But he tugged her back again, and soon they were making out with aggressive force.

Brutal kisses. Brutal caresses.

It didn't matter that their necks were craned in an awkward position or that another man was intimately involved. They couldn't stop the mutual madness.

For a split second, it was only the two of them.

Then she got a grip and brought Jay back into her mind. Desperate to come, she seated herself even more fully against him.

He didn't disappoint. He was aware of every rubbing, thrusting, catlike arch of her body. He sensed what she craved, what her sexual soul was crying out for.

He used fingers; his tongue; his mouth. He made her shiver from the top of her head to the tips of her crimson-polished toes.

All the while, she was fused to Luke. As he held the back of her body snugly against the front of his, she could feel his cock blasting through his jeans. She suspected that Jay was as equally aroused.

Two men. Twice as much power. Twice as much testosterone. Twice as much of everything.

The onset of her orgasm was blinding. Heat slammed through her veins, pulsing in fiery waves.

Amber accidentally bit Luke's lips and immediately stopped kissing him. She couldn't concentrate on anything except what was about to happen.

"That's right, baby," he said. "Come for us."

She didn't have a choice. She pitched into mind-blowing spasms, red and pink flowers blurring before her eyes.

The roses, she thought.

Dewy petals. Velvet softness.

Jay licked her until she lost all sense of reason and climaxed in a flurry, drenching him with her juices.

When it ended, Luke lifted her off of the other man, and soon she was snuggled between them.

Dreamy, she sank her head onto a pillow. Jay wiped the moisture from his mouth and smiled at her.

She smiled, too, thanking him for the pleasure he'd given her.

"This is going to be the best month of our lives," he said.

She couldn't help but agree. "It certainly seems so."

Steeped in her lovers, Amber stretched her long limbs. She was right where she wanted to be, cozy with both of them. Clearly they were giving her a break before the next hot-blooded round.

Maybe they would forget that they'd requested one-on-one time with her. Maybe they would let it fall by the wayside. It would be so much easier if they played as a trio, if everything they did was together.

In the silence, Jay shifted onto his side. "Did you know that Luke is working on a screenplay?"

"Really?" She turned toward Luke. "You're a writer?" As far as she knew, he was an actor and model, but apparently he had a literary gift, too. "What's it about?"

"I haven't actually started writing it. It's still in the research stage. But it's going to be about Curtis Wells."

She started. "My great-great-grandfather?"

He nodded, and she could do little more than stare. Since when had her family history become his concern or his interest or whatever?

She frowned. "Why would you want to write about him?"

"Why wouldn't I? His life was fascinating."

"Because he got himself killed over a woman?"

"He died for love. What could be nobler than that?"

There went Luke's romantic nature, punching her straight in the heart, stirring happily-ever-afters that didn't exist. During her bridal phase, she'd longed for that kind of love. But she'd wised up since then.

Amber said, "No one is worth dying for."

"Apparently she was."

She, Amber thought. Lady Ellen Fairmont.

A woman who could've married a duke, but ended up being the cause of a deadly duel instead.

"You shouldn't write about them," she told Luke. "You should leave them be."

"It's too late. They're already inside me." He tapped a hand to his chest. "I need to research their lives. I need to know exactly who they were."

"He was a gunsmith who was killed, and she was a scorned aristocrat who was sent to a convent after he died."

"I know. But I think there's more to them than that." He met Amber's cautious gaze. "So much more."

CHAPTER THREE

*The duke had me on one arm and Lady Milford on the other.
The closer we got to the stranger, the more anxious I became.
Lady Milford was anxious, too, but in a coquettish way.*

*Once the stranger became aware that we were headed
toward him, he excused himself from his companions and
stepped forward. Then he stopped and waited for us to ap-
proach him.*

*I wanted to drag my slipper-encased feet, but I couldn't.
Besides, I wouldn't have behaved imprudently when I was a
child, less a young woman betrothed to a wealthy and influ-
ential man.*

*The duke brought us directly to the stranger, and my pulse
fluttered at my neck. Heat radiated within my body, making*

me feel warmed by the sun. Only it was the moon that domi-nated the sky. I glanced at the terrace doors, wishing I was able to flee.

The duke said to the stranger, "I would like for you to meet my lovely fiancée, Lady Ellen, and her equally lovely friend, Lady Milford."

I had never actually considered Lady Milford a friend. To me, she was an acquaintance, but for the sake of the introduc-tion, I accepted our newfound friendship.

The stranger, who'd been identified as an American gun-smith named Curtis Wells, cast a polite smile upon us.

"Lovely indeed," he said in a slight drawl.

Or was it called a twang? I couldn't be certain, but I liked the oddly melodious sound.

In the silence that followed, he shifted his gaze from me to Lady Milford, then back to me.

She extended her hand in greeting and although he ac-knowledged her, I could tell that he was distracted by me. The secret between us made my heart pound. Why had I been so foolish as to steal admiring glances at him earlier? And why did he have to be so amused by it?

When I bit back my pride and offered to shake his hand, his smile turned devilish. But only for my eyes. No one else seemed to notice.

"Mr. Wells is my special guest," the duke informed us. "His

work is exquisite. I hired him to design a set of pistols. The most magnificent revolvers one could imagine."

I wasn't surprised. The duke collected firearms. They were his passion. He owned guns from all over the world. Commissioning custom pieces was well within his extravagant budget.

"How long will you be in Glenmoor?" Lady Milford asked the gunsmith.

"Possibly a month or more."

She thrust back her shoulders, allowing him to view her impressive bosom. Her décolletage was scandalously low, and she had quite the hourglass figure. Everything about her was voluptuous. Personally, I thought her rump was a little too big, but it wasn't her rump that was on display.

Still poised for attention, she queried him further. "So, what do you think of our little seaside country?"

"It's beautiful."

He looked at me, but only within the blink of an eye. He was crafty that way.

"I'm enthralled," he added, making me hold my breath. It wasn't our country to which he was referring, I was sure.

"We're a sovereign nation," she spouted, as if talking politics would make her more interesting. "Once ruled by England, but no longer." She patted her upswept hair, where jeweled combs shimmered. "What part of America are you from?"

"Texas, ma'am. But I've been just about everywhere."

"Ma'am?" She gave a girlish giggle, even if she was well beyond girlhood. "Now that does make you a Texan, doesn't it?"

He shrugged, but he laughed, too. So did the duke. I tried to seem humored, as well. But I fidgeted instead.

Fearful that my fiancé would notice my flighty behavior, I attempted to join the conversation.

"Sometimes I read about America," I all but blurted.

Mr. Wells turned toward me. "In what capacity?"

He seemed thoroughly interested in my reading endeavors, but what would he say when I revealed my book sources? My hypocritical father thought they were inappropriate for a young woman. Would he think so, too? And what of the duke? How would he react?

"It's nothing, really," I said.

Mr. Wells raised his eyebrows. "Reading about my homeland is nothing?"

Oh, goodness. "I didn't mean it that way. It's just . . . I just . . ." By now, I noticed the duke was frowning. There was no way out of this, not without making myself look the fool. "They're dime novels."

The gunsmith burst into a grin. "Well, now. A lady after my own heart. And which are your favorites?"

I grinned, too. Suddenly we were in our own world, just the two of us. I didn't even turn to see what the duke thought.

Nor did I bother with Lady Milford. "Anything about Jesse James. He was so daring. Robbing from the rich to give to the poor."

Mr. Wells chuckled. "Those stories aren't true. Jesse was a common thief."

I got indignant. "He was not."

"Yes, he was. It's all a myth."

Were my fantasies about Jesse James for naught? "Why would they make up stories about him?"

"To sell those novels."

He was still smiling at me, but more with his eyes than with his mouth. The twinkle in his dark gaze set my silly heart aflame. He made me feel like a schoolgirl.

"What other dime novels do you like?" he asked. "Besides the ones about Jesse?"

I tried to maintain my composure when all I wanted was to move closer to him. "Why does it matter, especially if there's no truth to them?"

"I just want to know."

"So do I" came a masculine voice from beside me.

The duke!

Oh, heavens. I'd forgotten about my fiancé. I turned to look at him, expecting to see disapproval. But he appeared to be intrigued by my dime novel habit. I relaxed a bit. But only a bit. I was much too aware of Mr. Wells and his effect on me.

I smiled properly at my betrothed and turned back to his guest, who waited for my response.

"I enjoy stories about cowboys and Indians," I told him.

"And which of the two do you root for?"

Dare I admit who I favored? Oh, why not. I'd already come this far. "I prefer the Indians." To me, their current plight seemed unfair, confined on reservations and whatnot.

There Mr. Wells went, grinning deliciously again. "The half-clothed heathens? Who would've guessed?"

Beneath my skirt, my frilly pink drawers turned warm, and I feared they would melt against the secret folds of my flesh. "You mustn't tease me this way. It isn't seemly."

"Sorry." He went serious. "I have some Indian blood in me. Comanche. But I don't run around half-clothed." He gestured to his well-cut suit, teasing me again. "I'm all buttoned up."

I tried not to picture him bared to the bone. Truly I did. But my mind stirred in the most sinful of ways. "You're wicked, sir." I looked to the duke for help. "He's wicked, Your Grace."

Charmed by the gunsmith he'd hired, the duke only smiled. "He's a product of the American West, dear lady. They're all a bit barbaric. You mustn't let it harm your delicate sensibilities."

If my betrothed only knew how harmed I was.

Suddenly Lady Milford sighed, reminding us of her presence. Clearly, we'd been neglecting her.

Mr. Wells shifted his gaze to her, flirting openly. "Surely you don't think I'm barbaric."

She preened under his attention, fluttering her lashes. "Actually, I do. But I quite like it."

"Well, then." He mocked a courtly bow. "Would you care to dance with a wicked American?"

Her cheeks bloomed with color. She looked simply radiant and a tad wicked herself. "I would love to."

They bid us a temporary farewell and glided onto the dance floor. I waited for Mr. Wells to glance back at me, just one more time, but he focused on the curvaceous widow and her décolletage.

"They make a dashing couple," the duke said.

"Yes, they do." Envy pummeled my heart.

"Come, my lady." He extended a hand to me. "Let us dance, too."

I behaved accordingly, following his lead. The duke was an accomplished dancer, and so was I. Regardless, I didn't think that we made a fetching pair.

As we waltzed, I scanned the other dancers, searching for Mr. Wells. When I caught sight of his broad back and longish hair, my body tingled.

I wished the duke made me feel that way, but my reaction to him was more sisterly or daughterly, I supposed. The thought of consummating our union made me ill. A woman shouldn't feel incestuous about the man she was to marry.

I peeked at Mr. Wells again. I could see the Indian in him. The half-clothed heathen, as he called it. Clearly his swarthy complexion and deep, dark eyes had come from his Comanche blood.

Did I have any dime novels featuring the Comanche? I wasn't sure, but I would rummage through my collection to check.

"You seem preoccupied," the duke said.

"Do I?" I asked absently.

"Mr. Wells didn't upset you, did he?"

I almost fumbled on the turn, correcting my footing before I made a spectacle of myself. "I was merely jesting about how wicked he is."

"No, you were right. He doesn't possess our breeding, but that's what I like about him. He's untamed, like the six-shooters he builds."

"It's fine. I'll get used to him."

"Good. Because we'll be seeing quite a bit of him. I offered him a suite in the Onyx Wing."

"He's staying here? At your estate?" Where I slept each night? Where my parents chaperoned me?

"There's plenty of room. Besides, I want to keep him nearby so I can watch the progress on my pistols."

"Of course, why wouldn't you?"

"Indeed."

As always, our conversation fell flat. We never found much to say to each other. I wondered if the duke had invited Mr. Wells to Glenmoor out of boredom. If anyone could add a dollop of spice, it was Mr. Wells.

Curtis, I thought, testing his given name in my mind.

"Did his reputation precede him?" I asked.

The duke nodded. Then his expression turned contemplative. "I apologize for not warning you ahead of time."

"Truly, it's fine. You don't need to inform me of your business dealings."

"I'm having your name engraved on the pistols."

"My name?" Now I felt positively sick about my attraction to the gunsmith. "You shouldn't do that."

He furrowed his brow. "Why not?"

Yes, why not? "Because Lady Ellen doesn't complement a pair of six-shooters."

"That's precisely why I'm having them designed that way. No one would expect it."

"Since when is unpredictability your style?"

"Since Mr. Wells suggested it."

"My name was his idea? Even before he met me?"

"He thought a titled lady's name on the guns would make them sizzle. Along with some roses and Western-style scrolls."

The discussion ended, with me going quiet. If I continued to protest, I would seem ungrateful.

Another waltz put us closer to Mr. Wells and Lady Milford. I studied the length of his powerful body, and when I glanced up to admire his profile, he turned in my direction and met my gaze.

Cursing my stupidity, I pretended that I was looking past him, but it was too late.

Once again, he'd caught me. But he didn't tease me, not this time. He simply looked back at me in a way that added a veil of mystery to his character, a romantic intensity that left me breathless.

~

Later that night, I struggled to sleep. I was in the Malachite Wing, and that put me one long winding corridor from the Onyx Wing, where Mr. Wells was.

Dare I climb out of bed and wander the estate? Would I be able to slip past his room undetected? Worse yet, would I be able to sneak past my parents' suite, which was only two doors from mine?

Probably, I assured myself. Most likely Papa wasn't even there. After the ball, he'd probably gone out carousing. It was *doubtful that he would be back before dawn. As for Mama, she no longer stayed awake, anticipating the return of her philandering husband. She'd learned to sleep through her distress. Nonetheless, leaving him wasn't an option. Since our emancipation from England, most of Glenmoor coexisted with less stringent beliefs, but Mama was philo-Catholic, as was Queen Victoria during the end of her reign, and Mama refused to consider a divorce, remaining faithful to her vows instead.*

Old and sad and faithful, I thought. Was that my destiny? The duke would never turn into a lecherous pig like Papa, but that seemed irrelevant in my case. Regardless of what a fine, upstanding man my betrothed was, I didn't love him, and a loveless marriage might steal my youth and happiness just the same.

I glanced around my suite, which consisted of a small sitting room, a decorative bed chamber and a private bathroom with modern conveniences.

My bed was draped with a lilac-colored canopy and the wooden posts were ornately carved. The lone tapestry on the wall depicted a country maiden straddling a stallionlike unicorn. The young woman's dress billowed in a magical breeze and golden locks flowed to her waist.

Every time I studied her image, I longed to become her, to disappear into an enchanted forest and merge with the moonlight.

I believed that she was riding off to search for the man who would set her free.

With that thought on my mind, I got out of bed and covered my embroidered nightdress with a silk dressing gown.

When my feet touched upon the floor, I was reminded of why this wing was called Malachite. Polished squares of the green stone were imbedded in an otherwise wooden covering.

The Onyx Wing, where Curtis Wells resided, had a similar design on its floors, comprised of the black marbled stone.

While fighting shallow breaths, I sat in front of the vanity table and unwound my plaited hair. Hoping to rival the maiden in the tapestry, I finger-combed the blonde waves trailing over my shoulders, giving them a windblown quality. I pinched my cheeks, too, adding a rosy hue to my nighttime complexion.

One last gaze in the mirror and I was ready.

With my feet bare, I crept out of my suite. As I passed my parents' quarters, I tiptoed and moved on. Scattered wall lanterns lit my way, creating ghostly shadows.

I knew this was wrong, but I needed to feel free.

Besides, I wasn't going to actually see Mr. Wells. Surely he would be asleep at this unholy hour, resting from the ball. He'd been the life of the soiree, dancing and socializing and entertaining other guests with his daring sense of self. Glenmoor's titled society would be gossiping about him long after he was gone.

I shook my head. Titled society? What foolishness it was. Now that we were no longer ruled by a monarchy, there was no longer a royal court. True, we had grandiose bloodlines, but in reality, we were merely figureheads.

Still, we remained respected. Even the new government, all of them elected officials, gave us a wide berth, allowing us to flaunt our titles.

Someday our stature in Glenmoor would diminish, but currently, our peerage still mattered. The duke often attended luncheons at the First Minister's palace, where he nibbled on cucumber sandwiches and played croquet. I, too, would be included once I became his wife.

If only unicorns were real, I thought, as I turned a quiet corner and landed in the Onyx Wing.

I had no idea which suite belonged to Mr. Wells, and even if I did, it wouldn't behoove me to stand outside his door in my dressing gown.

Making a crucial decision, I ventured toward the window at the end of the corridor. At least from there, I could gaze out at the world that was beyond my reach.

So there I went, walking softly to my destination. Some of the lanterns I passed had burned out, making the Onyx Wing darker than it should have been. But somehow that seemed fitting.

Once I reached the window, I gazed out at the view, which spanned a portion of the grounds. Beyond that was the sea. The forest was out there, too, and although it wasn't visible, I imagined it from my vantage point. Timbers, I thought, that grew tall and protective.

A haven for runaway maidens.

As a door behind me creaked open, I stood unnaturally still, praying that I hadn't been found out.

Yet I sensed he was there.

Curtis Wells.

Watching me from his doorway.

"Lady Ellen?" he said.

I tightened the front of my dressing gown, the silk clinging to my shuddering body. Suddenly I was cold. Or maybe I was hot, feverish in a way that tested my control.

I turned to face him and instantly noticed that he, too, wore his bedclothes, consisting of a cotton nightshirt and drawers. It was highly inappropriate for us to see each other this way, but he seemed completely relaxed in his attire. Me, I was nervous, but I'd brought this upon myself.

"Do you walk in your sleep?" he asked, giving me a legitimate excuse for being in the Onyx Wing.

I could've lied. Should've, I suppose. But I said, "I'm here of my own accord."

"To bask in the moonlight?" He gestured to the window.

"It's a compelling view. I stood there earlier, looking out at the sea."

"I was imagining the forest."

That gave him pause. "Why?"

"Because it's where I want to be."

"Then you should go."

"Now? In my nightwear?"

He smiled like the man of the world he was. "Why not? When I have the urge to flee, I make haste."

"Yes, but you're a loner. You wouldn't be leaving anyone behind."

His smiled vanished. "What makes you think I've never left anyone behind?"

I studied him in the low sketch of light. Now he seemed as dark as the Onyx Wing. Flecks of black penetrated his brown eyes. Were there shards of black in his wandering soul, too?

"It was merely an observation," I said. "Incorrect, I assume?"

"I rarely speak of this, but I have a wife and daughter. Former wife," he corrected.

My heart bumped my chest. "And you love her still?"

"No. But I love my daughter, and I miss her."

"What's her name?"

"Sophia. But we called her Sophie."

"That's a lovely name." Exotic, I thought. "How old is she?"

As he stopped to ponder the question, I realized that he hadn't seen his daughter in a long while. He appeared to be calculating the time he'd been away from her.

"She would be about eight now. Beautiful like her mother, I suspect." He leaned to one side and lowered his hand, creating what appeared to be the height of a toddler. "She was just a wee bit of a thing when I left."

"Why haven't you gone to see her? Why haven't you remained part of her life?"

"I wasn't around much to begin with. I preferred being on the road, peddling my guns, seeing the country, meeting new people. Even then, Sophie barely knew me."

I wondered if anyone truly knew him. Maybe I did, I thought. Because I understood his restlessness. Because I had it inside of me, too.

He continued to explain, "After the divorce my former wife remarried. Sophie has a new father now, a bookkeeper, a man who comes home each day." He glanced toward the window. "What good would it do for me to go back and confuse my little girl?"

I looked toward the window, too. I had no answer for him. But he didn't appear to expect a response.

Nonetheless, we'd just formed an unnatural bond—strangers confiding in each other.

Once the view lost its appeal, we faced forward. Instantly, our gazes locked. Struck by the connection, I reached out to brace myself against the wall. If I hadn't, I would've staggered like a willow in the wind.

"You're even more beautiful than the woman I married," he said.

"The woman you left behind," I countered, much too softly.

He stepped closer, but only by a margin. "Maybe some men aren't meant to settle down."

I stood where I was, longing to be touched by him, to be held, caressed, swept into the darkness in his eyes. "Maybe some women aren't, either."

His gaze had yet to leave mine. "Then I guess that makes us kindling spirits."

"Kindred," I corrected, pressing a hand to my bosom, struggling to still my fluttering heart.

"It's kindling," he insisted.

I considered his word choice. Kindling was the material used for a fire. Or the act of setting something on fire.

He was right. Oh, heaven, he was right. Heat burned between us. Emotional heat. Tender heat. Carnal heat.

"This is wrong," I said.

He made a wide gesture. "You came to me."

"But I shouldn't have."

"*Then go back to your sleeping quarters, Lady Ellen.*" Although he spoke gently, the timbre of his voice was rough. "*Go, and leave me to mine.*"

I didn't want to. But I knew it was the right thing to do. He knew it, as well. I could see the good in him, the sense of honor he wore like a damaged cloak.

We didn't exchange a parting phrase. A proprietary "goodbye" seemed off-kilter, and "Till we meet again" would have been worse.

Silent, I turned and dashed away, lifting the hem of my dressing gown to keep from stumbling.

I didn't glance back, but I knew he was watching. I could actually feel his fiery gaze upon my flesh.

By the time I entered my suite, I was shaking. I sat upon the edge of the bed and gripped one of the ornately carved posts. With my knuckles turning white, I stared at the maiden on the tapestry.

Hating her. Loving her.

Still wishing I could be her.

CHAPTER FOUR

Amber was looking at Luke, but somehow she was seeing Curtis. This wasn't her idea of fun. She didn't want to see her ancestor in Luke's eyes or in his heart or anywhere else.

"Will you help me with the research?" he asked.

She went flip. "Do I look like a historian to you?"

Jay answered from the other side of the bed. "You look like a girl who's afraid of feeling too much."

Caught off guard, she rounded on him. "As if you have room to talk. You probably still have feelings for your ex."

The normally casual Jay snapped back, "Don't make this about me, Amber. My divorce isn't the issue."

"Wow." Luke sat up and shook his head. "What did I do? What did I start?" He said to Jay, "Ease up, okay?"

He turned to Amber. "You need to ease up, too." He ran his fingertips along her waist and down her hip. "I just assumed that you would have some information."

Affected by his touch, she softened her expression. "I don't know anything about Curtis that isn't already out there."

"Maybe you do and you just aren't aware of it. Maybe there are family stories that you never paid attention to or belongings of his that you never took the time to examine."

She knew that Curtis's daughter had grown into a senile old woman, but what bearing did that have? As for Curtis's belongings, there was a pistol he'd designed that Amber's mother kept in a display case.

Hardly scintillating stuff.

"I'd rather talk about it another time," she said.

"That's fine." Luke trailed his hand across her thigh.

She glanced at Jay, and he leaned over to kiss her, obviously pleased that the three of them were back in good form. In spite of Jay's outburst earlier, he was ready to play.

After the kiss, both men stayed achingly close to her, making her feel soft and sleek and vulnerable.

Was this how Lady Ellen felt when Curtis was near? "I'm not like her," she said suddenly.

"And we're not like him," Jay responded, as Luke kept silent.

Amber wasn't sure what to think. All she knew was that

they were stripping off their clothes, and she was the object of their lust.

Fully naked and fully aroused, Luke sat on the edge of the bed. Jay did, too, and he was just as naked and just as erect.

With a deep breath, she knelt on the floor. This was the part where she pleasured them, back and forth, one right after the other.

She was excited, but nervous, too. "Who wants to be first?"

"Me." Jay opened his legs, eager for his turn. Or was he eager to torture Luke, to make his roommate wait? He'd lied when he'd said that they weren't like Curtis. Luke was, and everyone knew it.

Powerful. Intense. Romantic.

Clearing her mind, she settled between Jay's thighs and inhaled the masculine fragrance of his skin. Now wasn't the time to think about Luke's troubling qualities.

Jay's cock flared, and she grasped the root, preparing to give him what he wanted.

Her thoughts strayed. Was Luke watching?

She glanced in his direction. Of course he was. He couldn't take his deep, dark eyes off of her.

"Do it the same as before," Jay said.

She nodded. On the masquerade night, neither man had ejaculated during the oral phase of their foreplay. She hadn't done it long enough to make it happen.

It wouldn't be happening this time, either, at least not with Jay. What about Luke? Would he want to prolong his orgasm, too?

Focusing on Jay, she made feather-light swirls, teasing him, licking the head. She played with the slit, too, running her tongue along the opening.

He made an appreciative groan and tunneled his hands through her hair. For the fun of it, she nuzzled his testes, making them grow tighter.

She darted a glance at Luke, and his chest rose and fell with strong, choppy breaths. Was he imagining how it was going to feel when she did it to him?

Relaxing her throat, she went down on Jay. Inch by inch, the length and fullness filled her mouth. He thrust forward, and she used her hands to intensify the motion.

Amber liked the sensation, the heat, the aggressive rhythm. She liked kneeling between a man's legs while he lifted his hips and pushed deeper.

The saliva-drenched sound was sexy, too. Everything about it made her feel wildly feminine.

When she tasted a drop of pre-cum, she knew it was time to stop. Putting a gentle end to it, she released him and rubbed her cheek against his thigh.

"Sweet girl," he said, and they both smiled.

Now it was Luke's turn.

She sat up, and Jay told her to make his roommate "come all the way."

Heart pounding, she looked over at Luke. "Is that what you want?"

"God, yes." He had his hand pressed against his penis, as if he'd been fighting the urge to stroke himself, to come all over her.

Aroused by his excitement, she got in front of him. Then Jay changed the rules.

"Get on all fours," he told her.

So that was it. The reason he'd extended his orgasm. Amber wasn't about to disagree. She was more than willing to pony up. Or doggie up, she thought, considering the position Jay had requested.

Pleasuring two men wasn't easy on a girl, but Amber wasn't just any girl. This was her kink, what got her off, what kept her safe from commitment.

Eager to take Luke into her mouth, she got into position for Jay. She heard him behind her, tearing into a condom.

While she waited for Jay's penetration, she glanced up at Luke. As their gazes locked, every muscle in his beautifully sculpted body went taut. He scooted closer, and she noticed how long and thick his penis was, the same length and girth as Jay's.

If she closed her eyes and touched it, he could be either man. But she didn't want to close her eyes.

This wasn't good, she told herself. She shouldn't care so much about Luke, about absorbing his heart-sweeping intensity.

Since she was on all fours, she couldn't use her hands. Luke helped her along, holding his erection out to her. As she'd done with Jay, she licked the head, giving him a sexual shudder.

The man behind her said, "That's right," before he steadied his hands on her hips and plunged deep.

She keened out a moan and took Luke into her mouth.

He waited a beat, cupped her chin, then started to move, matching Jay's greedy strokes.

Such a wild sensation, to be fucked both ways. Already she was dizzy with it. By the time it was over, her jaw was going to ache and she would have rug burns on her hands and knees. But she didn't care.

Luke was lost in a lustful world. Her world. He stared blatantly where he entered her mouth, watching his cock go in and out.

Was her mouth warm? Wet? Slick? She'd always wondered how a man would describe the feeling.

Nasty, she supposed. Rough and sexy.

Jay tugged on her hair, adding another rough element. "Don't take your eyes off of him."

She wasn't. She couldn't. Luke was right in front of her.

Every so often he made eye contact, torn between watching the act she was performing and making an emotional connection with her. Desperate, he pulled her deeper between his legs.

Possession. Pure and primal.

He actually made her suck him all the way, to take as much as she could. He kept her down there, gripping the back of her head.

She realized now that Jay could watch, too. He could look over the top of her body and see that Luke was getting his rocks off.

Naughty boys, she thought, pushing back against Jay's aggressive thrusts. Soon they were all going to come.

The buildup. The pressure.

Who would it happen for first?

Behind her, Jay tensed, her question answered.

The ring leader was losing what was left of his sexual sanity. She could feel him, hard and heavy inside her, arching his long, muscular body.

Was he still watching her pleasure Luke? Or was his head tipped back? His eyes closed?

She didn't know. She couldn't tell. But his spasms ripped straight through her, making her come, too.

Trapped between two lovers, she gripped the carpet, nearly clawing her way through it.

Luke wouldn't let her off the hook. While she climaxed, he

pumped his hips, hitting the back of her throat and preparing for his release.

She cursed; she prayed; she went burning hot.

Jay shook one last time and emitted a long, low sound. Amber was shaking, too, her inner walls clenching around him.

When he pulled out, she was drenched. Not from him, but from her own slick juices.

In her delirium, she heard him removing the condom. Then Luke went off, the salty taste of him filling her mouth.

She had no idea how much she swallowed, but the white-hot wetness, the milky texture, almost made her come again.

When it ended, she sat up and caught her breath. Luke's legs were still open, his cock still half hard.

In the silence, he reached out and stroked her cheek, and they gazed at each other, soft and slow.

Before it got too emotional, she blinked and glanced away. In her peripheral vision, she saw Jay. He smiled and gave her heart a stop. To get away from him, she returned her attention to Luke.

Bad idea.

He could've been Curtis Wells looking at Lady Ellen. Confused, Amber stood up. She shouldn't give a damn about her great-great-grandfather or the woman who'd caused his death. She was related to Curtis through the child he'd abandoned— the one who'd gone senile in her old age.

"You okay?" Luke asked.

"Of course," she responded. "Are you?"

He nodded. His half hardness still hadn't gone away.

For a moment, she thought he was going to apologize for being so rough during the blowjob, but he didn't. Clearly he wasn't sorry for taking what he'd been desperate for.

She looked around for Jay and found him standing near the dresser, where the ever-present roses were—the gift from Luke.

Once again, silence engulfed the room. Talk about awkward afterglow. She pulsed with anxiety.

Finally, Jay shattered the quiet. "What do you say? Should we hit the pool?"

"Yes," she answered instantly.

She needed to dive into the water and cleanse her naked soul, to feel the sun on her back, to remind herself that this was nothing more than grown-up fun and naughty games.

～

Luke sat on the edge of the pool and watched Amber on the springboard. Tall and trim and naked, her all-over tan glimmered, making her look like the jet-setting goddess she was.

As far as he knew, Amber didn't work, at least not like the rest of the world. Sure, she was involved with her mother's company. Pia Pontiero, Inc., was a significant part of Amber's life, but not to the point of tampering with her freedom. Amber was the first to admit that she was spoiled. That she got whatever she wanted.

And what she currently wanted was Jay and himself. They were her male flavors of the month.

Whoosh!

She made an elegant dive into the water, glided below the surface like a mermaid and came up for air. As picture-perfect as a cosmetics ad, she smoothed back her sleek dark hair. Her face was damp, of course, but her mascara wasn't smeared. With her, nothing was ever out of place.

Did she ever cry? Or get a cold? Did her nose ever run? Was there ever a time that she was anything less than beautiful? He couldn't imagine it. Yet there was something that seemed off, the guarded part of her that Jay had mentioned—the girl who didn't want to feel too much.

He glanced over at Jay. He was just as bad. Sometimes that casual attitude of his seemed like a façade, especially after the way he'd snapped at Amber about his divorce.

Of course at the moment, Jay was all about Amber. He was watching her with lust in his eyes.

Damn, but Luke hated sharing her. Threesomes weren't his sex of choice. He'd only done it on the night of the ball because Amber had wanted it that way.

Same as now.

The whole thing was weird, especially since Luke and Jay cared about each other. They really were like brothers, even if Luke had denied it earlier.

He was envious, he supposed, because Jay had gotten to kiss Amber first. Cripes almighty, could he be any more juvenile?

Maybe the screenplay was making him feel this way. Maybe his attachment to Curtis and Lady Ellen was doing a number on him.

Whatever the case, he wasn't in love with Amber or half in love with her or whatever the hell Jay had accused him of being.

No way. No how.

He shot Jay another glance, and his roommate returned the look with a grin.

A fucking grin.

It made Luke want to punch him. In the next moment, a bare-assed Jay dived in the water, making a splash and meeting Amber in the middle of the pool for a hot, sultry kiss.

Luke was naked, too. Skinny-dipping. Apparently it was something that had been discussed earlier, before Luke had arrived home.

Screw it.

He jumped in, swimming over to them. Amber reached out and pulled him into the fold, and they kissed as well. Tongue to tongue, lust to lust.

The water was more cold than warm. In normal circumstances, his dick would've shriveled up to his balls. But with Amber's long lean curves pressed against him, his body temperature rose and he got a halfer.

Little sea witch knew it, too. She put her hand between his legs and teased him some more.

"I think we're going to need a condom," she said.

"No, we're not," he responded.

She lifted her brows. "Too soon for you?"

"Too crowded." He motioned to Jay, who rolled his eyes. Apparently he knew what Luke was up to.

"What's going on?" Amber asked.

Jay answered. "Luke isn't going to fuck you until he has you all to himself."

"Damn straight, I'm not." He'd agreed to a monthlong ménage, but as far as he was concerned, the specifics were up for grabs.

Amber glared at him. "You can't create your own rules."

"Too late. I already did." Their bodies were still pressed close. "So take it or leave it."

He half expected her to leave it. She looked ready to pitch a fit. But she relinquished, albeit childishly. She pulled away and splashed water at him, calling him an "ass" beneath her breath.

He didn't splash her back.

"You're going to be dying to be inside me," she said.

No doubt, he thought, but he was sticking to his guns.

Jay interrupted, changing the subject. "Is anyone hungry? I've got taco fixings in the fridge."

"Why not?" This from Amber. By now, she was climbing out of the pool and deliberately ignoring Luke.

He ignored her, too. To Jay, he said, "I can make a pitcher of margaritas."

Amber, the beautiful brat, pouted on a chaise lounge. But not for long. Suddenly she turned to both men. "We should play Truth or Dare after we eat." She flashed a winning smile. "With sexual dares, of course."

Jay and Luke were still in the pool. Jay raised his brows and muttered, "She's going to dare you to fuck her."

No shit, Luke thought. But he didn't want to "fuck" her. He'd already done that on the night of the ball. This time, he wanted to make love with her. He wanted her to mewl like a cream-satisfied cat, then curl up in his arms.

Just the two of them.

Frowning, he got out of the water, dried off and wrapped a towel around his waist, preparing to enter the house. As for the margaritas, he was going to make them stronger than usual. Luke needed the extra Cuervo.

When it came to Amber, his frustration never ended.

They ate poolside, seated at a patio table. The tacos were

smothered in guacamole, with chips, salsa and Spanish rice on the side. Jay whipped up killer meals. Luke mixed killer drinks, too. He moonlighted as a bartender to supplement his income.

"I've got a lease with an option to buy on this house," he said.

"Really?" That got Amber's attention. "You should buy it. It seems right for you."

"Glad you think so." He shoveled a few more bites of rice into his mouth and studied her.

Amber's hair had begun to dry and the towel she wore was tucked around her high, round bosom. On the night of the ball, she'd been dressed as a 1960s mod. She'd been wearing a long blonde wig, a micro-miniskirt, a see-through plastic top and go-go boots. Her glittering mask had been exaggerated with long spiky lashes.

He'd never seen a more beautiful creature. But he felt that way every time he saw her. Clothed or unclothed, blonde or brunette, she embodied his ideal. His fantasy. He imagined pouring his drink down the front of her towel and lapping her up.

Of course she would let him. Sex was Amber's game. The more men who worshipped her, the merrier she was.

She wet her lips, and his cock went raging mad. He hated the perpetual hard-on she gave him. It made him feel less in control of his life. At least Jay went flaccid once in a while. Luke ached every second he was near her.

If he were able to think with his brain instead of his dick, he would end the ménage and tell her to get the hell out of his house.

But he couldn't bear to lose her, not until he got her alone, not until he made some sort of decent sense out of what they were doing. There was something about Amber that waged a war inside him, and he was hard-pressed to define it. But whatever it was, sharing her with Jay only made it worse.

Amber pushed away her plate. Although she seemed to enjoy the food, she'd taken small helpings. He supposed it was a girl thing, the way she kept herself lean.

She divided her gaze between him and Jay. "Finish eating so we can play."

Jay chuckled. "Truth or Dare. This is going to be weird."

"It's going to be dark soon," Luke commented, as if the setting sun mattered.

"Perfect timing for us to play in the Jacuzzi," Amber countered.

She had an answer for everything, he thought, and in that glamorous accent of hers. He had a lingering accent, too. The evidence of his Mississippi roots.

"The Jacuzzi it is." Jay crunched down on the last of his

tacos. "A little naked game never hurt anyone." He glanced at Luke. "You might as well kick back and enjoy it."

Meaning what? That when Amber dared him to fuck her, he should do it, no matter the emotional cost?

Luke decided that his roommate wouldn't be so agreeable when truths or dares were being thrust at him. Since the one thing Jay didn't like to talk about was his ex-wife, Luke was going to make damn sure that her name came up.

In regard to Amber, he would find her weak spot, too. The part of herself she was guarding.

Rather than letting his companions know that he had ulterior motives, he flashed a smile that was more in keeping with Jay's personality than his own. He stood up and adjusted his towel. "I'll go fire up the jets, and as soon as it's hot and bubbling, we can get started."

"That's my boy." Amber sipped her margarita. "We're going to have oodles of fun."

More than she could possibly know, he thought. As far as he was concerned, nothing was off limits.

If this game of hers didn't kill them, it was going to make them stronger.

One way or the other, they were destined to find out more about each other than they ever expected to know.

CHAPTER FIVE

I slept fitfully, and in the morning I contemplated what I knew about Mr. Wells and what he knew about me. In actuality, very little. Yet it seemed like a lot.

We'd shared something forbidden last night. Something deep. Something emotional. What would it be like to take those forbidden feelings even further?

"Shall I draw your bath?" Miss Morgan asked.

My heart bumped my chest, and I turned to look at her. For a silly moment, I'd forgotten that she was in the room. Miss Morgan was a lady's maid, provided, of course, by the duke. She was younger than I was, maybe all of nineteen, with pale skin, curly red hair and a sprinkle of freckles. Regardless of her youth, her high-ranking domestic position earned her the privilege of being referred to as Miss Morgan, rather than Esther, which was her given name.

Silent, she waited diligently for my response.

"Yes, thank you," I finally said. "I'm ready for my bath."

She nodded and went about her duties, unaware of my despair.

On this troubled morning, I longed to confide in her, to share my intimacies, but I kept quiet. Still, I couldn't help but wonder if she had secret fantasies, if there was a young man who made her feel forbidden.

Steeped in last night's endeavor, I considered Mr. Wells. Was he up and about at this early hour? Had he gone to the stable for a ride? Or was he lounging in his suite, waiting to greet the day?

Surely, he would join us for the morning meal. Breakfast was served promptly at the same time each day. The duke ran an orderly household. When we were married, I would be expected to oversee it in the same precise manner.

Just the thought made me melancholy.

Miss Morgan returned. I thanked her and entered the bathroom, where the curtain-draped tub had been filled with warm, lightly perfumed water. She waited for me in the bed-chamber, as she knew I preferred to bathe alone.

I pinned my hair loosely to my head, removed my night-dress and climbed into the tub. The water caressed my naked-

*ness, and I sighed from the luxury of it. But as I began to wash
my body, I got a chill.*

A sexual yearning.

*I struggled to ignore it. I wasn't prone to performing illicit
acts on myself. I'd been taught that it was immoral, and I believed this to be true.*

*But what about the maiden on the unicorn? A woman like
that would find no shame in pleasuring herself.*

My cheeks went hot. Should I do it? Could I do it?

*Of course I could. No one would know. I was alone in the
tub.*

*A soap-laden fantasy crossed my mind. What would it be
like to have Mr. Wells bathe my body? To feel his hands upon
me?*

*Falling prey to my own deviations, I leaned back and
imagined that he was touching me, running the soap over my
breasts, across my stomach and lower ...*

Lower ...

*I washed intimately, lathering my most private region,
back and forth and up and down.*

With a sweet sigh, I rinsed clean.

*But it wasn't enough. I wanted to keep imagining that he
was with me, so I closed my eyes and used my fingers.*

Yes, there. At the junction of my thighs.

Shameful as it was, I couldn't seem to stop my wicked foray.

I stroked myself, making soft little circles, creating gentle pressure. I even lifted my bottom in the air, as if I were presenting myself to him.

Such wanton behavior. Would I behave that way in reality? I opened my eyes and glanced down. By now, my body was gloriously arched and my legs were scandalously spread.

I kept rubbing, making myself feel good. Making myself feel bad.

I'd heard naughty secrets, rumors that wild-hearted men sometimes kissed their lovers down there. Would Mr. Wells do that to me? I tried to envision such a thing.

Was it regular kissing or the French type?

Shocking myself silly, I gasped. I had no right to let my mind stray in that direction. Yet I pictured Mr. Wells kneeling between my thighs, showering me with warm, wet, tongue-lashing kisses. To intensify the image, I rocked forward, sloshing the water.

Heaven on earth.

My muscles went unbearably taut. My bottom rose higher in the air. I bit down on my lower lip to keep from crying out. Flames licked my skin, searing every sinful inch of me. I oozed with lust, with disgraceful pleasure, with life-spinning heat.

This was wrong. So very wrong. But my flesh knew no morals. I bucked and shuddered like the virgin harlot I was fast becoming.

Sensation after sensation rammed into me, and I feared I was being punished. By the time it ceased, I barely had breath left in my lungs.

Mortified, I drew my knees up. I wanted to cry, to rage, to scream, to lock myself away in a tower where no one would find me.

How could I be betrothed to one man and be immorally enamored of another? Two men should never be part of a woman's equation. Yet it had become my deepest, darkest, most painful dilemma.

Somehow, I would have to turn it around. I would have to abandon my attraction to Mr. Wells and give my hedonic heart to the duke.

Determined to comply, I stepped out of the tub and dried my bared body, careful not to touch myself in a tingling way. My nipples, God help them, remained peaked and sensitive.

After slipping on a dressing gown, I waited for the aftermath of my shame to disappear, then returned to the bedchamber so Miss Morgan could help ready me for the day.

"I want to look exceptionally nice," I told her. "For the duke." Not for Mr. Wells, I added mentally.

"Yes, of course." As I sat at the vanity table, she paused to study me in the mirror. "Your betrothed is lucky to have you, Lady Ellen."

Would she have said that if she'd known what I'd done in

that bath? And who I'd been thinking about when I'd done it? Certainly not. No one would consider the duke lucky to be engaged to a woman fighting lustful feelings for another man.

Once we chose my wardrobe, I put on my undergarments, and she went to work on my person, making me rival the demurest of damsels. She styled my hair with curling tongs and an array of pins. For the final touch, she adorned my upswept curls with a pink bandeau dotted with tiny silk flowers. On the outside, I was angelic. On the inside, my identity faltered.

No matter how hard I tried to forget him, Mr. Wells lingered in the back of my sullied mind.

Foolishly I asked, "Have you met the duke's new guest? The American? The gunsmith?"

"Not officially." Miss Morgan took my question literally. "There would be no purpose for me to meet him."

"But you've seen him?"

"Yes. Briefly." She lowered her voice. "He reminds me of Billy. Only older."

"Billy?" I wasn't sure who she meant.

"He's one of the stableboys."

"Ah," I said, becoming aware. He was the dark-eyed, dark-haired one. Of course to Miss Morgan, he would not be a boy at all. They were most likely the same age.

When I looked at her, she glanced to the floor. Clearly, Billy was her forbidden fantasy. Or maybe he was more than that. Maybe he was her secret beau.

I was dying to know, but didn't dare ask. Not today, not after I'd imagined Mr. Wells as my secret beau.

She retrieved my dress, and I stepped into it. As I fastened the front buttons, she tied the decorative bows in back. The daytime fabric was cool and creamy, and the bottom ruffles swished around my ankles.

In the quiet, my heart pounded beneath my breastbone. Romantic images of her and Billy crowded my mind.

"How old do you think he is?" she asked.

"Billy?" I queried, getting confused.

She brought me my slippers. "No, my lady, not Billy. The American."

Not as old as the duke, I wanted to say. "Middle thirties, I would guess."

"Like Lady Milford?"

"Yes."

"Did she flirt with him at the ball?"

"Yes," I said again. "That's what I heard."

So the gossip had already begun, pairing Mr. Wells with the buxom widow. Better her than me. My family couldn't afford the scandal.

My thoughts wandered. Would Mr. Wells rendezvous with Lady Milford? I hoped not. I couldn't have him, but I didn't want her to have him, either.

Miss Morgan glanced at the wall clock, with its walnut case and gold pendulum. "It's almost time for the morning meal."

"Oh, goodness." I'd dallied for far too long in the bath, leaving limited time for the rest of my toilet.

We hurried, adding a single strand of pearls to my neck and a touch of rouge to my cheeks.

"You're enchanting," she said.

"Thank you." We exited my suite and she veered off in another direction, leaving me to myself.

I took to the hallway, then began descending the sweeping staircase, preparing to see the duke and be the devoted fiancée I was meant to be.

As I descended lower and lower, my fate came into view.

At the foot of the stairs, the duke waited for me. As always, he was prompt and impeccably groomed. I don't think he'd ever been late or disheveled.

Mama was there, too, also waiting for me. They both turned to watch me walk down the last set of stairs, as if I were a bride making her way to the altar.

Papa, of course, was nowhere in sight. Most likely, he was sleeping off the cheap ale he'd drunk.

The duke smiled and greeted me, telling me how lovely I

looked. *So did Mama. I thanked them, then took a moment to study my mother.*

She was thin, too thin, with graying blonde hair and a complexion that always seemed to be lacking color. Her eyes were blue, like mine, but they'd lost their sparkle long ago.

I got the painful urge to hug her, to comfort her, but that would've been awkward.

"Shall we?" I asked, inviting the duke to escort Mama and me to the breakfast room.

"No, my lady, not yet," he responded. "Mr. Wells will be joining us."

"Oh, of course. I should have realized."

Trapped in clock-ticking silence, the three of us waited for the gunsmith. I had no idea how long we would be expected to stand there. Would Mr. Wells appear within a reasonable amount of time?

If not, what would the duke do? As far as I knew, none of his guests had ever been notoriously late for a meal. None save for Papa, and he didn't count.

Luckily, Mr. Wells didn't keep us waiting beyond the duke's patience. Or maybe it was unluckily. I would've preferred that the American not show up at all.

Yet there he was, handsome as ever. He came down the stairs wearing a dark gray daytime suit, only his tie remained loose. He wasn't quite put together.

"*I'm sorry I'm late,*" he said to all of us.

As his gaze slipped past mine, I held my breath.

"*Not to worry,*" the duke responded. "*Shall I provide a manservant for you in the future?*"

"*Oh, you mean for this?*" Mr. Wells fingered his tie. "*I've always hated these things.*" He grinned and pretended to choke himself with it.

Clearly, the American's antics amused the duke. My betrothed chuckled. As for Mama, she eked out a ladylike laugh. And why not? She'd probably imagined hanging Papa a time or two.

I released the pent-up air in my lungs. That was the best I could do.

Mr. Wells removed his tie and slipped it into his pocket. "*If no one minds,*" he said as an afterthought.

If it had been anyone else approaching a meal in such an informal way the duke probably would've minded. But bohemianism was part of the gunsmith's charm, and no one, not even the duke, desired to quell his nature.

Of course I'd been exposed to another side of the American. The lonely side. The tragic side. The man who didn't know how to be a husband or father.

The duke offered his arm to Mama, allowing Mr. Wells to escort me. I suspected that my fiancé was hoping that I would become comfortable in the other man's presence. If only the duke was aware of what had transpired last night.

As Mr. Wells moved toward me, as our arms linked, as his body heat radiated against mine, I put one foot in front of the other and warned myself to look straight ahead.

"Relax," he whispered in that Texas tone of his, only making me more nervous.

"Don't reprimand me," I whispered back.

Kindling spirits, he and I. All I wanted was to be with him. In all sorts of romantic ways.

Romantic ways? Like in my shameful bathtub fantasy?

Never again, I thought, as I gazed at the duke and my mother, who were several paces ahead.

Finally, the four of us reached our destination. The duke held out a chair for Mama, and Mr. Wells followed suit for me.

The breakfast room wasn't as vast or as grand as the formal dining room, but it was elegant in its own way. Glass doors provided natural light and offered a view of the garden, where acres of brightly colored flowers flourished.

The table had been beautifully set, with fine-boned china, lace-edged linens and crystal goblets.

A kitchen maid served coffee, tea and juice, then returned with stewed fruit.

I wished that I had more of an appetite. Instead, I picked at the first course. More was soon to follow. The second would be porridge and milk. The third would consist of bacon, fried eggs, grilled tomatoes and mushrooms. It never, ever varied. It was the combination the duke preferred.

"Where will you be setting up your shop?" Mama asked the gunsmith.

She was accomplished at small talk. Normally I was, too. But this situation was different.

He answered Mama. "The duke built a shop for me, my lady. Just west of the carriage house."

"How wonderfully thoughtful of him." She acknowledged my fiancé with a nod. Then back to Mr. Wells, she said, "You must take my daughter and me on a tour of your workspace."

Oh, goodness, I thought. How in heaven's name was I supposed to avoid him if everyone kept involving me in his visit?

"I'd be honored," he told her. "But I'm still getting settled. As soon as everything is in its place, you'll be my first guests."

I nibbled on a fig and sighed inwardly from relief.

Continuing the conversation, Mama spoke again. "Is it true that my daughter's name is going to be engraved on the pistols?"

"That's absolutely true." He smiled, flashing his roguish manners. "And in the prettiest script imaginable."

"How exciting." She beamed in a way I rarely saw.

What an effect he had on women. My mother, the fading

countess, almost seemed young again. She, of all people, was surrendering to his spell.

So where did that leave me? Fighting even harder to keep my distance? To not crave his proximity?

I stole a glance at the duke. He sat proudly, as if he were responsible for the gunsmith's charm. And in a way, he was. He'd brought Mr. Wells to our little country.

The second course arrived, and I battled the urge to watch Mr. Wells eat his porridge.

After what he'd done to me in my fantasy, was it any wonder that his mouth was a source of fascination?

Blast the duke for bringing him into our lives. How was I supposed to survive my feminine yearnings?

I tasted my porridge and added more honey. But it didn't sate me. I wanted to pour the creamy sweetness down the bodice of my dress and let it saturate my skin.

Like an ancient body mask, I thought. An erotic beauty treatment. Nothing in my head made sense.

Mr. Wells had a strong appetite. By the time the third course arrived, he was devouring his first English-style breakfast and enjoying every bite of it.

He continued conversing with Mama. The duke joined in and although the three of them chatted about inconsequential things, they enjoyed each other's company.

I sat there like a ninny. Where were my social skills? My breeding? My schooling? My ability to rise to any occasion?

Finally the meal ended, and I hoped that I would get a reprieve. But my discomfort worsened.

Mama excused herself to tend to her needlepoint. On her way out, she smiled at both men, but her smile lingered a tad longer on the American.

If she'd been twenty years younger, she probably would have run off with him. Or at least considered it.

Was that what I was doing? Considering him for my escape?

After she left, the duke said to me, "I'm going to be engaged in business for the next few hours. But we can spend the afternoon together, if you'd like."

"Thank you, Your Grace. That sounds lovely."

"It would be my pleasure." To Mr. Wells, he said, "Would you mind entertaining my fiancée for the rest of the morning? Before you set up shop?"

I wanted to protest, but it would have been improper for me to balk at the duke's suggestion. Besides, I suspected that my betrothed was trying to prod me into accepting the American's uncivilized ways. Aside from my expressed interest in Wild West novels, I'd treated the duke's special guest like a leper.

Or so the duke probably thought.

Mr. Wells responded, "I'd be happy to entertain her. Maybe a walk in the garden?"

"That will do nicely" came the other male response. "The garden is one of her favorite spots on the estate."

I stood there, cinched into my corset, listening to them arrange my morning. Such was the plight of the fairer sex, I thought, wanting to give them both a swift kick.

Before Mr. Wells was given full permission to whisk me away, the duke took me aside so we could speak privately.

"Walking with him will be good for your spirits," he told me.

"What if he does something inappropriate?" I asked, hoping to trick my way out of this.

"He won't."

"How can you be sure?"

"I can see his honor, my lady. If he were one of us, he would be a knight."

Like Sir Lancelot? I wondered, keeping my lip buttoned. King Arthur hadn't been a naïve man, and neither was the duke, but the story was starting to feel familiar.

That kind of trust was perilous, I thought. But I understood why the duke viewed Mr. Wells in a positive light. I'd seen his honor, too. Last night in his eyes.

"I'll educate him about flowers," I said.

The duke fissured a smile. "I'm sure he'll be charmed."

89

I backed away from my fiancé. "Until this afternoon, Your Grace."

"Until then." He gestured for Mr. Wells to escort me outside, and that was that.

I was in the gunsmith's dangerously noble care.

CHAPTER SIX

Luke climbed into the hot tub with his companions, and the water bubbled around their naked bodies. Naturally, Amber sat between Jay and himself. On the side of the Jacuzzi were a handful of condoms. Protection, Luke thought, the wrappers bright and shiny.

By now, dusk had fallen, and the moon peeked through the sky, creating silvery hues.

"We need to set some house rules before we start the game," Amber said.

Jay slicked back his unruly hair then flashed a slow grin. As always, he was being his good-natured self. "I haven't played Truth or Dare since middle school."

"I think it was elementary school for me." Luke turned to

Amber. "Everyone has to agree on the rules." He wasn't going to let her make all the decisions. Not when he was trying to use the game to his best advantage.

She leaned back against the Jacuzzi wall. Below the surface of the water, her breasts became more visible, making his body stir. He cursed his lack of self-control.

"Okay," she said. "But the first rule has already been established, so no one can change it."

"Yeah, I know. Sexual dares only." Luke was going to pick truth each and every time.

"What's the next rule?" Jay asked.

"The dares can only be performed here. In the hot tub," she clarified. "With all three of us present."

Luke shrugged and uttered, "Fine." If he chose truth every time, it didn't matter.

"What about the questions?" Jay asked. "Do those have to be sexual, too?"

"Yes," she said.

"No," Luke countered. "Anything goes with the questions." Otherwise, he wouldn't be able to delve as deeply as he intended.

Amber squinted at him. Clearly she wanted this to be an erotic game, and he was spoiling her party-girl fun.

"You're a pain in the posterior," she told him.

Jay chuckled. "She's got you there."

"Oh, yeah?" He leaned over to make eye contact with his roommate. "Keep it up and I'll dare you to kiss my hot little posterior."

"No, please. Not that." Jay chuckled a bit harder. "It would be like kissing my own ass."

"That's true." Amber laughed, as well. "Even I can't tell the difference in the dark."

"Listen to you two, a couple of clowns." Unable to help himself, Luke nibbled on Amber's shoulder, reprimanding her in a foolishly gentle way.

She sighed before she batted him away. "No physical contact without a dare."

He wanted to keep nuzzling her, but he couldn't. So he pushed the game forward. "Ladies first."

She contemplated his offer. "First to respond to truth or dare? Or first to ask it?"

"To ask. But whoever you pick gets picked by the next person, too. That way, we all get a chance to question each other."

"Or dare each other." She sat forward and her breasts popped out of the water.

She stared straight at Luke, and he waited for her to pick him. But she turned away and chose Jay as her first conquest.

"Truth or dare?" she asked him.

"Dare." Apparently he was in the mood for some naughty fun, especially from Amber.

She smiled and dared him to suck her nipples, to nurse them so hard, they went from pink to red.

Luke frowned. On the night of the masque, he'd been known as "Red" and Jay as "Pink" in reference to the color of their boutonnieres. And now, it pertained to the glorious torture of Amber's nipples.

He hoped that he hadn't made a mistake, agreeing to an adult version of an adolescent game. He didn't want to watch what was about to happen, but not watching seemed like an even worse option.

As Jay latched onto one of Amber's breasts, she made a sweet sound and tugged him closer.

He sucked and sucked, over and over, fulfilling his dare. Every so often, he would release his prize to check its color. Finally when it was red enough, he nursed her other breast.

Amber moaned from the pain, from the pleasure, and her expression drove Luke half mad. The way she bit down on her bottom lip, the way she drew it roughly between her teeth.

When it ended, she drifted back against the Jacuzzi and immersed her body, soothing her nipples under the jet-streamed water.

"Your turn," she told Luke, reminding him that Jay remained the subject of the next truth or dare.

"Dare me to do something else to Amber," Jay said.

Yeah, right. As if. "Maybe I should dare you to do something to me."

The other man wasn't amused, particularly when he flashed back to their earlier conversation. "I'm not kissing your ass."

"Then you'd better pick truth." Because one way or another, Luke was determined to manipulate the game.

Amber balked at him. "You're not playing fair."

"Kissing my ass is a sexual dare."

"Not for Jay."

"Can I help it if he's straight?"

"So are you," she snapped.

He ignored her logic and addressed Jay. "So, are you picking truth?"

A snarled "Yes" was the reply.

Finally, things were going Luke's way. Breaking the intimacy, he moved to the other side of the Jacuzzi so Amber wasn't nestled between two naked men.

Luke's question was a doozy. Quickly, he sprung it on his roommate. "Are you still in love with Beverly?"

Jay flinched, and Amber's curiosity piqued.

"Is Beverly your ex?" she asked Jay.

He nodded, but he didn't respond to Luke's question.

In the interim, Luke waited, and so did Amber. Clearly, she wanted to know the answer. Luke wondered if he should be jealous, if her interest in Jay meant more than it should.

Too late to backpedal. He'd already put it out there. "You picked truth," he said to Jay. "So tell us the truth."

The other man blew out a tight breath, and Amber reacted, scooting closer to him. So close, Luke wished he hadn't moved to the other side of the Jacuzzi. Suddenly he felt uncomfortably alone.

"I don't know," Jay finally said.

"You don't know what?" Amber queried.

"If I still love her."

Luke wasn't sure what to think. Was Jay being deliberately evasive? "How can you not know if you love someone?"

"You asked for the truth, and that's it."

"Sounds like you're taking the easy way out to me."

"Oh, yeah?" Going all mad and manly, Jay thrust his chin. "What about you and Amber?"

Luke's testosterone elevated, too. "What about us?"

"You don't know if you love her."

Oh, fuck, Luke thought. That again. "I already said that I didn't."

"Because you don't know the damned difference."

"Amber isn't my ex-wife, Jay."

"No, she isn't. But you look at her the way I used to look at Beverly."

Caught off guard, Luke merely sat there. Amber didn't

fare much better, except that she moved away from Jay, as if he'd just betrayed her.

Luke finally came up with a retort. "Of course I look at her the way you looked at Beverly. Beverly is insanely gorgeous, and so is Amber."

Jay's ex was an exotic dancer, but Luke kept quiet about that. He figured that Jay could mention it if he wanted to.

Of course, he didn't. The former husband went silent.

"Have you met Beverly?" Amber asked Luke.

He shook his head.

"Then how do you know she's gorgeous?"

"I saw a picture of her." In the *L.A. Weekly*, he thought, in an ad for the club where she worked. Jay had told him her stage name, so she'd been easy to recognize. "Believe me, she's hot."

"Hmm," Amber said, making Luke wonder what she was thinking.

A moment later, Jay climbed out of the Jacuzzi, but he didn't go back in the house. He retrieved the margarita pitcher from the patio table and refilled his glass.

"Any one else want one?" he asked.

"No, thanks." Luke figured the leftover drink was watery by now, something that didn't seem to matter to Jay.

Amber declined, too.

In the silence, Jay returned to the Jacuzzi and resettled into the bubbling water, cocktail in hand.

"Are you done grilling me now?" he asked Luke.

"It was only one question."

"One you knew would pack a punch."

Touché, Luke thought. But Jay had gotten in a significant jab of his own. That crap about Luke loving Amber.

"Let's get back to the game," the margarita man said.

Moonlight glinted off of Amber's hair. "You still want to play?"

"Hell, yes. I've got a truth or dare for my roommate."

In response, Amber shot Luke a look that said, *It's your turn*. Beautiful and smug, he thought. But her time would come.

"Truth or dare?" Jay asked Luke.

Naturally, he picked truth.

Adding a bit more drama to the game, Jay took his time, finishing his watery drink. Then he asked, "Why are you so idealistic?"

Luke squinted at his accuser. "What kind of question is that?"

"A good one," Amber injected, prodding him to respond.

To explain, he supposed, why he was writing a romantic screenplay. Or why he gave women flowers. Or why he wanted to make love with Amber without the presence of another man.

"I guess I was raised that way," he said.

"By who?" Amber wanted to know.

"My mom. But mostly it was my three older sisters who tried to influence me. They were always talking about how girls wanted to be treated. They told me silly bedtime stories, too."

"Fairy tales?" Jay asked.

Uncomfortable, Luke scoffed. "Yes, but I didn't liken myself to the heroes." Not with his rough moods. He would rather ride a dark ghostly steed than a big white stallion.

"What happened to your dad?" Amber asked. "Why wasn't he in the picture?"

"He died when I was a baby."

"I'm sorry," she said.

"My Choctaw blood came from him." The way Curtis's Comanche blood had come from his father.

She trapped his gaze. "Let me dare you, Luke."

He shook his head. He wasn't going to get seduced by her. Not here. Not like this. He knew better than to give her that kind of control.

"Just a kiss," she told him.

Once again, he shook his head. If he agreed, she would end up initiating more. "I'm not doing any dares."

She studied him for a moment, and he wondered if she was going to quit the game. But she didn't. Instead, she posed a truth question, asking if he had an ex-wife or an ex-girlfriend or anyone from his past who mattered.

He answered, "There's no one," and glanced away before Jay accused him of feeling too much for her.

Just to be sure, he caught his roommate's gaze, and the other man lifted his brows, but said nothing.

Determined to move on, Luke returned his attention to Amber. "It's your turn to be in the hot seat."

"Then I'm picking dare," she challenged, leaving him with a dilemma. What kind of sexual dare was he supposed to create that wouldn't affect him?

Should he dare her to kiss Jay? A soft and simple kiss on the lips?

Hell, no, he thought. He didn't want to watch them get romantic, not after they'd accused him of being idealistic.

How about daring Amber to touch herself?

Oh, sure, as if that wouldn't make him big and painfully hard.

He sat back in the Jacuzzi, racking his troubled mind.

She huffed out a breath. "*Luke.*"

"Hold on. I'm thinking."

"About what? How to cure world hunger?"

He ignored her sarcasm, then got a brainstorm. "I dare you to become another woman and describe what you look like, using your own body as a guide."

For Luke, it was a way to detach himself from her, and for the time being, he needed to lessen the attraction.

"Interesting idea." Luckily Amber seemed intrigued, but she liked masquerades, and in a sense, that was what he was asking her to do: to play dress-up, but without her clothes.

"It's different," Jay said. "Not as sexual as I would've liked, but I'm sure Amber will add some spice."

"Of course I will." She stood up on the Jacuzzi seat, flashing full-frontal nudity.

Luke watched her and so did Jay. It was impossible not to. She commanded their undivided attention.

"Let's see," she said. "I think I should be a California blonde, and my hair should be long and luxurious."

"Like the wig you wore at the ball?" Luke asked.

"Yes, but not quite that straight. It should be thick and full with big bouncy waves." She used her hands to demonstrate.

Luke glanced at Jay. The other man was riveted to every word. Then Luke realized what was happening. Beverly was that kind of blonde.

Amber went on. "Her boobs should be bigger than mine." She cupped her breasts and exaggerated the fullness. "Her waist should be narrow." She ran a hand down the flatness of her stomach. "And she should have a navel piercing and wear a precious jewel in it."

"A diamond," Jay said, barely taking a breath.

"Yes, a diamond." Amber smiled, clearly enjoying his input.

Luke tried to recall the photo he'd seen of Beverly. She had a pierced navel, didn't she? There was no way Amber could've known that. By sheer instinct, she was conjuring Jay's former wife.

All too soon, the tortured ex-husband would be pulling Amber into his arms. Luke could feel the sexual energy, the heat pumping through his roommate's blood.

"She should have a dark, glowing, all-over tan, and her pussy should be fully waxed." Amber opened herself up, exposing her vulva and her pretty pink clit.

The naughty description went on and on, with Amber demonstrating each intimate body part.

It was all too much. As predicted, Jay approached Amber and dragged her against him.

They kissed and caressed, with Luke watching them. He cursed himself for the dare he'd created.

Jay eased her down, and she sat on the edge of the Jacuzzi and opened her long, luscious legs. Desperate, he tore open a condom, sheathed himself and slid inside.

Deep and slow.

The tempo increased, and she arched against him, taking him full-hilt. He pleasured her with hip-pumping strokes, and Luke imagined that he was in Jay's place.

Only Luke wouldn't be thinking about another woman.

Would Amber care if she knew that Jay was fantasizing

about his ex? Or would she accept it as part of the game? The masquerade scenario?

In the midst of the heat, of the hunger, she looked up at Luke, and his heart hit his chest, making him realize how emotionally damaged all of them really were.

Truth or Dare, he thought. On a desperate summer night.

～

At bedtime, Luke lay beside Amber, assessing the situation he was in. She seemed sated, and so did Jay. At the moment, Jay was in the shower, but he'd enjoyed his twisted evening. Or so Luke assumed. He'd watched the other man come inside of Amber. Twice. What could feel better than that?

She turned to look at him, and he struggled to calm his quickly beating heart. She looked soft and sultry-sweet. For some girlish reason, she'd decided to wear a sheer nightie to bed. She was naked underneath, and the peek-a-boo design tightened his loins.

"It's just us," she said.

"Not for long. Jay doesn't take wasteful showers."

"He conserves water?"

"He tries to. We both do."

"You're green men."

He couldn't help but smile. He knew she meant environmentally conscious, but it made him think of flying saucers and wonderfully bad B movies with little green guys in ill-fitting martian suits.

"You're hot men, too."

He stopped smiling. "I wasn't. Not tonight." He hadn't touched her or kissed her or held her. He'd wanted to, but he hadn't.

"You watched. That was hot, Luke. The way you stared at me when Jay was doing his thing."

"Yeah, both times."

"I know. My God. I've never seen him so turned on. It only took a few minutes for him to get hard again."

Envy rammed his gut. To combat the feeling, he lashed out, "It wasn't that miraculous. He was thinking about Beverly."

"What?" She blinked at him.

Wishing he'd held his temper, he tried to take it back. "I didn't mean to say that."

"Too late. You already did." She leaned on her elbow, her expression annoyed or confused or somewhere in between. "Did he tell you he was thinking about her?"

"No, I just assumed."

She wouldn't drop it. "Because you mentioned her earlier?"

"Because you described yourself as looking like her. The tall, tanned, bouncy-haired blonde with the big tits and navel piercing. That could've been Beverly."

She scrunched up her face. "Really?"

He nodded and made a face, too. "It was weird."

"You shouldn't have made me do that."

"How was I supposed to know that you were going to describe her?"

"I was describing half the strippers in Hollywood."

He made another face. This was getting weirder.

She gauged his reaction and widened her eyes. "Please don't tell me that Beverly is a stripper."

"She is. An exotic dancer." He considered the term. "I always thought it should be *erotic* dancer, though."

"Dang. That isn't what I expected." She remained on her elbow, leaning in his direction. "What's your opinion? Do you think he still loves her?"

"I don't know. But after the way he reacted, I'd say that he's still hurting over her."

"Where does she work?"

"At The Dusky Doll."

She shifted completely onto her side and scooted closer. Close enough for him to inhale her soft, citrus perfume. He almost leaned over and kissed her.

Until she said, "We should go watch her dance."

"Seriously?"

"We'll ask Jay to go with us."

"Yeah, like he's going to go for that."

"It might help get her out of his system."

"By taking his dirty little ménage to her club?"

"We're more than that," she said. "We're his friends, too."

Her response surprised him. But he never knew what to make of Amber. She was as complex as a cat with nine lives.

She returned to her agenda. "So, do you want to see her dance?"

"I've always been curious about her. But I'm not going to the club. Not unless it's okay with Jay."

"We'll talk to him about it tomorrow. I think the wife wound is too fresh tonight."

After that, neither of them said anything. He couldn't explain why. Maybe they just needed the silence. Or maybe the wife wound was weighing heavily between them, too.

Since they were still unbearably close, he finally took the liberty of kissing her.

As his lips touched hers, he savored the feeling. They kissed and kissed, but it wasn't enough. Desperate for more, he slid down her body, raised the hem of her nightie and spread her slick folds. He wanted to kiss her there, too.

With a lustful moan, she lifted her hips, and he devoured her musky-sweet flavor.

She caught her breath. "Jay is going to walk in on us."

"I know." And for now, he didn't care. As much as he wanted her, this wasn't the time to dwell on being alone.

Right on cue, the door opened and Jay entered the room, squeaky clean from his shower. He climbed onto the bed, and Luke accepted their threesome for what it was.

He offered her to Jay, and they took turns, making her come against their tongues. Together, they gave Amber what she wanted.

Intimacy in an uncommitted way.

CHAPTER SEVEN

Amber sat at the kitchen table. Wrapped in a robe, she watched Jay fix breakfast. While he made pancakes, Luke lorded over the coffee. Both were dressed in blue jeans, with no shirts and no shoes.

"Who wants to go shopping with me later?" she asked.

They turned at the same time, reacting to her question. Luke smoothed his straight dark hair. He had the warrior vibe going this morning. The sun slashed through the window, highlighting his cheekbones and shadowing the hollow ridges beneath them.

"Shopping for what?" he asked.

"Clothes," she responded.

His incredulous look matched Jay's. Apparently they

weren't interested in accompanying her on a charging spree.

Without further ado, Jay returned to the pancakes, and Luke poured a cup of coffee and placed it in front of her. She added artificial sweetener and frowned at him. He smiled and bent down to kiss the top of her head. The warrior had gone gentle.

Instead of reacting favorably, she shot him an annoyed look. Was he trying to make her all gooey inside? Amber didn't like the feeling.

"What's wrong?" he asked as if he had the right to weaken her defenses.

"Nothing." She tasted her coffee. He'd made it too strong, but she drank it anyway.

"Is she pissed because we won't go shopping with her?" Jay asked without even glancing over his shoulder.

Luke responded, "Who the hell knows."

The other man laughed. "*Women.*"

Yes, women, she thought. "Actually, I should be mad at you, Jay."

"Me?" He spun around. "What did I do?"

"You thought about Beverly when you were with me in the Jacuzzi. Why didn't you tell me that I was describing her?"

He went stone-cold silent, and from the other side of the kitchen, his roommate winced.

"Sorry," Luke said.

Jay rounded on him. "Sorry, my ass. You were goading me with that truth crap."

The warrior got his back up. "Maybe I was, but that doesn't make you any less obsessed with your ex."

Before a major fight broke out, Amber rejoined the conversation. "Luke and I talked about going to The Dusky Doll to watch Beverly dance and we want you to go with us."

Behind Jay, a pancake was burning. "Whose asinine idea was that? His?"

"No. Mine." She gestured to the pan. "You'd better get that off the fire."

He grabbed it and threw it in the sink. "I'm not going with you."

"Come on." If anyone understood being mired in the past, it was Amber. "You need to purge her from your system."

Jay rubbed his hands across his face. He was starting to seem less angry, and he wasn't the type to stay mad.

Finally, he blew out a sigh and said, "You're right, I do. But not by watching her dance. That's what caused our divorce. I couldn't handle her job."

Amber quickly asked, "Did she become a dancer after you married her?"

"No. Weird as it sounds, I met her at the club. In the beginning it was fun dating a stripper. But after I fell in love with her, after I married her, after she became my wife, it felt different."

"You got jealous," Luke said, as if it made perfect sense to him.

Jay nodded. "All we did was argue about it. But I still wanted to be with her. I couldn't let go. I guess I'm still having trouble with that."

Amber sipped her too-strong coffee. "I take it the divorce was her idea."

"Completely." Jay turned to rinse the pan.

In the silence, Amber glanced at Luke, and he glanced back at her, neither of them knowing quite what to do.

Luke spoke up. "We won't go to the club."

Jay turned back around. "No. It's okay if you do."

"Are you sure?" Luke asked.

"Positive. You can fill me in. You can tell me how she is and what you think of her."

"We will." Amber couldn't deny her curiosity. She was dying to see the ex-wife Jay couldn't seem to forget.

Returning to chef mode, he served the pancakes. The stack that hadn't burned was golden brown.

Soon everyone was eating, sitting at the table together, like the twisted family they'd become.

Luke waited for Amber in the living room. He was dressed and ready to go, and she was taking her sweet time. But if he knew her, she was laboring over every detail. Amber was fanatical about her wardrobe.

Click. Click. Click. High heels on hardwood floors. Finally she appeared.

If Luke had been one of those cartoon dogs, his tongue would've lolled out of his mouth.

She wore an electric blue jumpsuit-type thing, slinky as all hell. The top part was shaped like a tank top, with a keyhole design that buckled across her nearly exposed breasts, enhancing her cleavage and leaving her stomach bare. The pant portion fit equally tight, clinging to long, shapely legs. She was already runway-model height, and her spiky shoes put her at over six feet tall and eye level with him.

"Wow," he said.

"You like?" She turned, making a sleek pirouette.

"Yeah, I like." Even her makeup was spectacular: flawless skin, vogue eyes, lush red lips. She could've stepped out of the pages of a sex-kitten catalog.

Curious he asked, "Is that called a catsuit?"

She nodded, and he acknowledged the reference in his mind. He'd already been thinking of her as feline.

She glanced around. "Where's Jay?"

He motioned to the patio. "Taking in the night air."

"Thinking about Beverly, no doubt. We should say good-bye to him before we go."

They opened the sliding glass door and walked onto the patio. Jay was still seated at the table. He turned to look at them.

"Wow," he said, reacting to Amber the same way Luke had when he'd first seen her.

She tried, once again, to prod him into seeing his ex. "Last chance to join us."

He stuck to his guns. "No, thanks." A second later, he said, "Beverly does a bride routine. It's her signature act. All of the girls at The Doll wear costumes. Bev's is this sexy little wedding dress, with white stockings and garters and all that."

In the picture Luke had seen of her, she'd been attired in white lingerie. The underwear that complemented her costume?

Jay blew out an audible breath. "What a bride."

No one responded for what seemed like the longest time. Then Amber finally spoke. "I wanted to get married when I was younger. In fact, it's all I wanted."

Both men turned to look at her, and she quickly waved away her comment. "It was just stupid kid stuff."

Luke wasn't going to let it pass, not that easily. Clearly, Amber had just revealed a guarded part of herself.

He said, "My sisters used to plan their weddings. They even picked out their dresses, using pictures from magazines."

"Really? So did I. Only I designed it myself, looking through Mama's pattern books and making sketches. It was an oyster-colored satin sheath." She made a sweeping gesture. "With a pleated Watteau train."

"What about your bouquet? Did you design that, too?" He smiled. "I'll bet long-stemmed roses would have looked good with it."

"Luke." She shook her head. "You and your flowers."

He shrugged, tried to act casual. "So what happened to your wedding dream?"

"I changed my mind after I got a realistic view of marriage. My mom was married four times and they all walked away. All of them, including my biological dad."

Luke wanted to reach out and hold her, but she'd already taken a step back.

Jay, who'd been quietly listening, rejoined the conversation with a simple, "That sucks, Amber."

"So does marriage," she reiterated.

"I can't argue with you there."

She sighed, then laughed. "Maybe we ought to get married and change the rules."

Jay angled his head. "We?"

She made a circular motion, including Luke. "The three of

us. Two grooms and one bride. A fake ceremony with a really dirty honeymoon."

Christ, Luke thought, his breath slamming from his lungs to his throat. "You're kidding, right?"

"Actually, I think it would be fun. Our wildest ménage ever. We could do it at a hotel room."

Jay joined in. "We could say dirty vows, too."

Luke gaped at him. "You actually want to do this?"

"Why not?" Jay popped off with a grin. "I need to let go of my ex, right? Get her out of my system? So I might as well get 'remarried' and have a nasty honeymoon. What could be more purging than that?"

Was Luke the only one who hadn't lost his mind? "You two are making a mockery out of something that's supposed to be beautiful."

"It's just a game," Amber said. "A little feel-good farce. Besides, we can make the setting beautiful. We can have cake and champagne. And I'll wear the dress I always wanted to wear, and you guys can wear tuxedos."

Luke merely gaped at her again.

She stood there in her catsuit, with her hand on her hip. "If you don't want to participate, Jay and I can do it without you. Of course then it wouldn't be a threesome, but I'm sure we'd still have fun."

Fun, my ass, Luke thought. No way was he going to let

them take vows without him. Dirty or otherwise. "Fine. Whatever. I'll do it, too."

"Then it's settled." Amber smiled. "A wedding ménage. Is everyone free this weekend?"

"I don't have to work," Jay responded.

"Me neither." But Luke wished that he did.

"Then I'll make the arrangements." Amber smiled again. "The wardrobe. The hotel. Everything."

Yes, everything, Luke thought. That shouldn't be happening.

━

The Dusky Doll was located in a two-story building in the San Fernando Valley, an eclectic area of L.A. where Soccer Moms drove SUVs and the porn industry filmed a majority of their movies.

Upon entering the club, Amber looked around. The walls were pearly pink and the furniture a combination of dark wood and crushed velvet. The stage, equipped with a long brass pole, was in the center of the main floor, with tables and chairs positioned around it. The second story was reserved for private dances.

The clientele was mostly men, but there were a handful of other women, too. Amber got plenty of attention, plenty of admiring stares, but she'd planned it that way.

The music was loud and lively, and the rowdy girl on stage was in the process of peeling off her cheerleader gear, but only as far as a G-string. The Dusky Doll was a topless bar, not a full nude.

Scantily clad performers were dressed in a variety of ways, each with a naughty persona. Amber noticed a cowgirl, a dominatrix, a beauty queen, a princess, an eighties rock star, a forties pinup, a medieval wench . . .

Some were giving tables dances, some were having drinks with customers and others were walking around in their skimpy costumes, soliciting dances.

"Where do you want to sit?" Luke asked.

"Over there." She indicated an area with a cozy view. They'd already checked the lineup and Beverly, whose stage name was Malibu, wouldn't be performing for about an hour.

They occupied a table, and a cocktail waitress appeared with prompt and friendly service. Luke went for a draft beer and Amber chose a Climax, a combination of liqueurs, vodka and cream.

Their drinks arrived, and Luke put them on a tab, leaving the bill open. When the cocktail waitress left, he swigged his beer. Amber sipped from her glass.

"Is it good?" he asked.

"Not as good as you'd probably make." He was, after all,

moonlighting as a bartender. He knew his climaxes, in and out of bed.

He turned toward the stage, and she sat back in her chair. Was she doing the right thing? Planning a wedding ménage?

Yes, she thought, she was. Jay admitted that he needed a new wedding and honeymoon, and Amber needed to turn those old bridal dreams into something wild and fun.

In terms of Luke . . .

He would make an exceptional groom.

Was that why she'd created this scheme? To fantasize about being married to him?

No, of course not, she told herself. It was all about the sex. The naughtier, the better.

"We should make it a masquerade," she said.

He turned back to her. "What?"

"Our wedding and honeymoon night. You and Jay can be made up to look exactly the same. Like at the ball." She'd been itching for another masque and this was her chance to make it happen.

"You want to put us through that again? Why?"

"So I won't know which groom is which." So it didn't matter if she was his bride or Jay's. "It'll be hotter that way."

"It won't work, Amber. You'll know who's who."

"Not if you use the same accent, like you did at the ball.

Not if you become the same man, not if you throw yourselves into your roles."

"How can we when Jay's willing to have sex with you during a threesome and I'm not?"

She mulled over his point. "Then we'll make it a foreplay night. No sex, other than oral. We can use toys, too. Lots of erotic devices."

He conceded. "Okay, but I still think you'll know who's who." He leaned over and kissed her, softly, then a bit roughly, as if trying to isolate his identity.

Could she tell the difference if Jay kissed her in the same possessive way? On the night of the ball, they'd seemed like the same man. But what about now that she'd gotten to know them?

He pulled back, leaving her heart crammed in her throat. Breathless, she said, "I'll pretend if I have to."

"That you can't tell us apart? That's cheating."

"Not to me." She turned to see who was on stage. A naughty nurse in a sheer white costume strutted her stuff. When she untied the front of her itty-bitty dress and flashed her tits, the patrons at the tip rail tossed dollar bills at her.

"She's making them feverish," Luke said. "Of course so are you. Do you know how many men in this place keep stealing glances at you?"

"Does that make you jealous?"

"Not if you don't return their stares."

"I'm more interested in the show." Florence Nightingale was a blonde with big fake boobs. "Is that what Beverly looks like?"

"Beverly is prettier. Classier."

"I guess we'll see."

"You don't trust my opinion?"

"Maybe you're only enticed by her because she used to belong to Jay."

"And maybe we're just attracted to the same type of women." He leaned over for another hot-blooded kiss.

Once again, he left her reeling. Would a second Climax help? It wasn't fair that the taste of him lingered on her lips.

Afterward, they sat there, steeped in half-naked dancers and loud music.

"I wonder if she uses any props," Luke said. Clearly, he meant Beverly.

"Like what?"

"I don't know. Wedding stuff."

"Like a bouquet?" She hoped Beverly wasn't carrying flowers or tossing petals out to the crowd. Red roses, of course, would be the worst.

The one thing Amber wasn't going to include in her wedding night with Luke and Jay was flowers.

She'd gotten more than enough roses from Luke already.

CHAPTER EIGHT

I walked beside Mr. Wells in the garden, but I couldn't think of anything to say. Neither, it seemed, could he. As my hand accidentally brushed his, I could feel the uncomfortable warmth between us. If he were my fiancé, I would have made the touch linger. But I drew back, curling my fingers into my palm.

Finally he spoke. "The duke said this is your favorite spot on the estate."

"It is." Normally the colorful setting gave me peace. "I usually come here alone."

"It seems endless."

"It does." Leafy plants and artful blooms as far as the eye could see. "I told the duke I would educate you."

"About what?"

"Flowers." I made a grand gesture, where cosmos and marigolds grew. *"But I doubt my ramblings would charm you. The duke said they would, but—"*

"Your betrothed is right." He turned to meet my gaze, his eyes dark and alluring. *"I'm interested in whatever you have to say."*

My heart went pitter-pat, tapping like rain upon my chest. *"Are you familiar with Queen Guinevere?"* I asked, venturing into a realm in which I shouldn't.

"King Arthur's wife? Why?"

Because once again I was reminded of her love affair with Lancelot. *"She was more than a queen. She was and still is a goddess and one of her roles as a goddess is as a Flower Maiden."*

We stopped walking, and Mr. Wells stood beside a sweet pea plant, where the scented vine climbed along a tall white trellis.

"What does that mean?" he asked.

"It means she brings fertility to the earth."

"Then do you think she's here?" He seemed intrigued. *"Making all of this grow?"*

"She could be." I tried to imagine her, with braided hair and the palest of skin, dressed in grass-green silk. *"She would be beautiful, I think."*

He skimmed his hand along the trellis, following the sweet pea. *"Like you."*

"I'm not Guinevere." Even if I was torn between two men,

even if I understood her plight. *"I'm no queen. No goddess, either."*

"You'll be a duchess. To me that's a queen. And all beautiful women are goddesses."

We were treading upon shaky ground. Not literally, of course. But my legs could've wobbled just the same. I didn't tell him that the duke had compared him to a knight or that I was likening him to Lancelot. I wasn't brave enough to mention Guinevere's affair. But it didn't matter, I told myself. She and Lancelot hadn't remained together.

As a quiet moment passed, Mr. Wells released the trellis and reached out, as if to touch my cheek, but he never made contact. He dropped his hand instead. He knew better than to get too close.

Clearly we both did. To avoid further incident, I resumed our stroll, although it was anything but leisurely. Tenderness shifted between us. So did a mounting breeze, blowing the curls that created my coiffure.

"Teach me more," he said.

"About what?"

"The Flower Maiden and how you think she affects this garden. What do you think her best loved plants are?"

"Hawthorn trees are sacred to her." I pointed to a dense area beyond our sight. *"The wood can be used for making talismans and wands."*

"It's magical?"

"So they say. But it's pagan to believe that way."

"I believe in magic. I'm a white man with Comanche blood. I can't help my pagan ways."

What was my excuse? I wondered. *The Arthurian Legend? My sudden attachment to a queen who'd betrayed her husband? Now the maiden on the unicorn seemed suspicious, too. Was she Guinevere in another of her goddess forms?*

"Will you take me to the hawthorn trees?" he asked.

"They're too far from here." The magic had begun to scare me. The magic in the air. The magic of being in his company.

"Then show me the rose garden." Before I could inquire about his interest in roses, he added, "They're the flowers I'll be engraving on the duke's pistols."

"Oh, yes, of course." Along with my name. I wasn't happy about his request, but at least the rose garden was only a short distance away.

I guided him in the direction of where we needed to go, which took us past a mixture of candytufts and daisies.

When we came upon a perennial with pleated foliage, he asked, "What is this called?"

"Lady's mantle."

He stopped to study it. "Because the leaves look like a lady's cloak?"

"Yes." The dew that collected on them was said to be magi-

cal, but I didn't want to discuss yet another source of magic with him. "The roses are just ahead." And I needed to keep moving.

The breeze intensified, rustling my hair once again. My dress blew against my body, too.

"Are you chilled?" he asked. "I can give you my jacket."

"I'm fine."

"Please. I insist." He removed his jacket and draped it across my shoulders. "Now you have a mantle."

Although I clutched the fabric as if it were a cloak, I wasn't able to change the masculine shape of it.

By the time we reached the rose garden, I felt heady from having his garment pressed intimately against me.

"This is quite a display," he said.

"Yes." I inhaled the floral scent, still fighting the sensual warmth of being wrapped in his jacket. "Some are wild and some are cultivated."

"What color pleases you the most? And don't say all of them." He teased me with a Southern smile.

My pulse quickened. He never failed to affect my vitals. I gazed at the array of roses, assessing each delicate hue. "I'm undecided between pink and red."

"I'd choose red for you."

"And why is that?"

"Because my wife favored pink, and I'd rather see you with red."

Then so would I, I thought.

He removed a pocket knife from his pants and cut a crimson bloom from its bush. I watched as he trimmed the thorns, making the flower safe to hold.

When he handed it to me, I thanked him, holding it close to my rapidly beating heart.

I didn't tell him that red roses embodied love and passion. It seemed better left unsaid.

Yet, as we stood there, looking longingly at each other, he seemed to become aware of what his gesture meant.

A gesture, I feared, that would lead me to his bedchamber that very night.

~

Every time Amber glanced at Luke, images of red roses cluttered her mind. Crimson petals.

Was it any wonder she needed Jay? To keep her grounded, to be her other groom?

"What time is it?" she asked Luke.

He checked his watch. "It's almost ten."

Almost time for Beverly to hit the stage. "Should we sit at the tip rail?"

"If you want to."

"I do." Because she wanted to see Beverly up close, to look into the other woman's eyes and see her soul, or at least an inkling of it. "Do you think we'll be able to tell if she regrets divorcing Jay? Or if she ever really loved him?"

"How would we be able to tell something like that?"

"I don't know."

Regardless, they got up and moved. Once they were settled at the tip rail, occupying two side-by-side seats, Luke pulled a fast one and kissed her, the way he'd been kissing her all night.

Was he trying to take her mind off of Jay? Or was he merely staking his usual claim?

While his tongue swept her mouth, Amber closed her eyes, and suddenly there was nothing but him. No music. No bumping and grinding on stage. No other patrons.

He pressed closer, and she got warm and wet between her legs. Beneath the barlike counter of the tip rail, he was playing with her belly button through the keyhole of her catsuit. She imagined taking his hand and pushing it past the fabric so he could rub her clit.

When the kissing stopped, she opened her eyes and stared at him.

"I want to take you on a date," he said.

"We're already out together."

"A real date. This doesn't count."

It felt uncomfortably real to her. "I don't want to talk about it right now."

"Then when?"

"After our wedding night." She would feel stronger after the double-groom ménage.

He made another playful stab at her belly button, dipping his thumb into the indentation. "Do you want to go with us to pick out the toys we're going to use? Or do you want to be surprised?"

At the moment she didn't know. Her mind was cluttered again. "I need to think about it."

In the next instant, Beverly's name was announced. No, not Beverly. Malibu. The stage name of Jay's former wife.

Luke faced forward and so did Amber. Was his pulse pounding? At his throat? At his cock? Was he aroused by the notion of the other woman?

Was Amber? Between the toy talk and the anticipation of Jay's ex, her pulse was pounding, too.

As the Divinyls' version of "I Touch Myself" blasted from the DJ's booth, Beverly took the stage looking more beautiful than an altar-bound stripper had the right to.

She wasn't carrying a bouquet, but her white lace micro-minidress and virginal veil were enough to seal the bridal deal.

She moved with grace and style, elegantly accustomed to her platform shoes. Her legs were naturally long and shapely, with ladylike stockings attached to garters. Beneath her dress was the sequin-trimmed outline of a bustier, where the tops of her breasts spilled out.

Amber was dying to see her face, but Beverly didn't remove the veil.

Not yet.

She circled the stage, stopping every so often to tease the audience, to touch herself, mimicking the lyrics of the song.

Proving herself an experienced pole dancer, she climbed her way to the top and spun her body around, making her dress whirl.

Was it possible that she'd been born to strip? Everyone had a gift and this appeared to be hers.

With skill and sensuality, she performed acrobatic moves. In appreciation, catcalls sounded and dollar bills flew onto the stage.

Her dismount was even sexier. She slid down, slowly, softly, caressing the long gold bar like an erect penis.

Amber couldn't seem to stop herself. She put her hand on Luke's fly and discovered how hard he was. She rubbed him through his pants, and he turned to look at her, erotic emotion in his gaze.

Realizing how public their display of affection was, she pulled her hand back. From there, they both focused on the stage.

The dancer tore off her veil and let it flutter to the ground.

Stunning green eyes came into view. Beverly had the features of a siren.

Continuing to strip, she removed her dress, exposing her sparkling bustier and ribbon-enhanced G-string.

Like the pro she was, she got down and crawled along the rail, keeping time with the song. She went from patron to patron, allowing them to tip her, up close and personal.

When Beverly crawled over to Luke, she started. Not enough to damage her show, but enough that Amber noticed. Clearly his resemblance to Jay had thrown her for a loop.

Amber knew the feeling.

Luke stuffed a five down the bride's bustier, and she quickly moved away from him. Instead of completing the tip rail circle, she got back on her feet.

In a moment of vulnerability, she met Amber's gaze, curious, it seemed, to see the woman who was with Jay's cosmic twin.

Amber knew that feeling, too. Or understood it, at least. She would've done the same thing.

Beverly glanced away before too much of a connection was made. She still had a routine to finish.

With bad-girl finesse, she bared her breasts, licked the tips of her fingers and wet both nipples. She ran her hands along her stomach, too, grazing her pierced navel.

Once again, money flew onto the stage.

Amber watched closely, waiting to see if Beverly risked making eye contact with Luke. Although the stripper didn't tempt herself, her dilemma was clear. She looked in every direction but his.

As the song came to a close, she gathered her clothes and cash, winking at a few smitten patrons. She even chanced another look at Amber. Yet she avoided Luke with every naked beat of her heart.

After she disappeared behind the stage, Amber and Luke remained quiet. Finally, they agreed that they should go home.

And never, ever come back.

~

Luke sat in the living room with Amber and Jay. All three were staring at the TV, where a rerun of *Big Love*, the HBO show about a modern-day family practicing polygamy, was in progress.

Of all things, he thought, to end their night.

Amber had changed out of her catsuit and into a simple white tank top and a pair of drawstring shorts. Curled up on the couch while he and Jay sat in separate chairs, she sipped a cup of mint tea.

Moments like this weren't in Luke's emotional sphere of a three-way relationship. Amber looked natural, homey in a way that made her seem like somebody's cozy wife.

Somebody's? His? Jay's?

Both, he supposed, considering the wedding and honeymoon they'd agreed upon.

Luke shifted in his chair. So far, they hadn't discussed Jay's ex. But they were about to.

"Beverly did her bridal routine," Luke said, his Southern voice shattering the Utah undertones on the show.

Jay met his gaze. "What'd you think?"

Luke wasn't about to lie. He put the TV on mute. "She's good. Hell of a pole climber."

The former husband made a mocking laugh. "Yeah, I know."

Amber placed her tea on an end table, still looking like somebody's cozy wife. She turned toward Jay, telling him what he needed to hear. "Beverly wouldn't even make eye contact with Luke. I think she recognized his resemblance to you."

"Really? So seeing a guy who looks like me bugged her, huh?" He seemed please that his ex might be as tortured as he was.

"I can see why you miss her," Amber said. "She's very erotic."

Jay left his chair and came over to the couch. "Yeah, but who needs her when I have you?"

As he kissed Amber, Luke turned uncomfortably jealous.

In the background, *Big Love* remained on mute, flickering like a silent movie.

Without hesitation, Jay lifted Amber's tank top, baring her breasts and making her nipples peak. It was so easy for him to be with her. When he wanted her, she was there for him, always willing, always eager. Their affair made sense.

Luke wanted to walk away, but he stayed where he was, no matter how envious he felt.

Jay removed Amber's shorts and peeled her panties down, tossing them in Luke's direction. They landed at his feet, but he didn't pick them up.

The foreplay continued. Jay used his fingers inside of Amber and when they got wet and sticky he brought them to his mouth and licked each digit clean.

Luke imagined that he was able to taste her juices, too.

Soon she was spread out on the couch, and Jay was discarding his clothes and rubbing himself between her legs. He hadn't strapped up with a condom yet, and the cock to cunt motion battered Luke's libido.

They kept rubbers all over the house, making protection easily accessible, but apparently Jay wanted to prolong the ungloved ecstasy.

Frustrated, Luke undid the front of his jeans, just to ease the pressure.

Jay finally went for a condom, grabbing one from the

trinket box on the coffee table. Within seconds, he was sheathed and thrusting inside her.

Amber moaned and clutched the other man's ass, leaving nail marks on his skin.

Luke gave up the fight and freed his cock. Amber turned to look at him, and he rubbed his thumb across the tip. He liked that she was watching.

While they stared at each other, while Jay fucked her, Luke spit into his palm and stroked himself. It felt wrong; it felt dirty, but he couldn't stop the urge.

In fact, he retrieved her panties and used them for his pleasure, rubbing the silky fabric against his painfully erect penis.

By the time this was over, he was going to defile her panties, and she damn well knew it. But it excited her, the way it excited him. He saw the raw hunger in her eyes.

Jay glanced up and noticed what was happening. He only smiled and fucked her harder. He didn't care if she was watching Luke get nasty. But then why would he? He was eager for their wedding ménage. He'd already accepted her as their naughty bride.

Jay lifted Amber's legs, pushing them forward so he could increase the rhythm. It made Luke stroke faster, as well. He'd never jerked off in front of anyone, but he was too far gone to end the madness.

Pornographic sounds escaped Amber's throat, heightening her sudden climax. Jay pounded into her, using his long, taut body like a jackhammer. He was coming, too.

That was all Luke needed for his trigger. He pumped himself into lust-driven oblivion and ejaculated all over Amber's pretty little panties.

During the act, she remained beautifully fixated on him, making him want to do it again and again.

Afterward, he cringed at the white-hot mess in his hand. Somewhere between the wedding plans, the strip club and TV polygamy, Amber had become his downfall. His Lady Ellen, he thought. The woman destined to destroy his sanity.

And everything that went with it.

CHAPTER NINE

While in the warmth of my bed, I lifted the rose on my nightstand from its vase and placed it gently on the pillow beside me. Should I go to Mr. Wells? Should I offer myself to him?

Troubled, I looked up at the tapestry where the maiden on the unicorn was headed toward her fate. Was she Guinevere? Or was my imagination at work?

The prudent thing would be to remain in bed, to draw the covers up and remind myself that I was betrothed to the duke, that my future had already been arranged.

But I was no longer a sensible woman. I wanted to make love with Mr. Wells. I wanted to feel his bared body next to mine. I wanted the hardened length of him inside me.

I climbed out of bed, dizzy with wants. Would he be wait-

ing for me? Or would I have to slip into his suite and awaken him?

I walked over to the vanity and stood in front of it. Then, without taking time to rationalize my behavior, I removed my nightdress. I shed my undergarments, too.

There, naked in the mirror, I gazed at my reflection. Was I fetching enough? Would I compare to his other lovers? He'd already told me that I was more beautiful than his wife. Had he spoken the truth? Or had her beauty only diminished in his eyes? Would he love me more than he'd loved her?

Was it possible? Did men fall in love during affairs? Of course, I soothed myself. Lancelot had loved Guinevere. He'd been exiled because of her.

And what would happen to Mr. Wells if our union should be discovered?

Most likely, the duke would have him banished from Glenmoor. As for me, my family would lose the financial benefits the duke provided, and my reputation would be soiled. But I didn't want to think about that. Not now.

I chose a dressing gown from my wardrobe and slipped it on. I wanted to be naked save the delicacy of an easy-to-remove garment.

Should I unbraid my hair or allow Mr. Wells to do it? I decided that I wanted the pleasure to be his, so I loosened the plaits a bit, hoping to make his romantic endeavor easier.

Was I losing my mind? Manipulating the loss of my virginity? Yes, I was. But I needed Mr. Wells. I needed him beyond measure.

I glanced at the rose on my bed. For the most part, the duke had reacted favorably to it. He thought it had been kind of Mr. Wells to give me a fresh bloom, but even so, he'd expressed his concern that it hadn't been cut and trimmed properly. Regardless, my fiancé suggested that I keep it in water until it wilted.

I intended to do more than that. Before the flower lost its complete luster, I would press it inside of a heavy book, and once it dried, I would hide it amongst my dime novels for safekeeping.

Just one more act of trickery, I thought, to burrow with the rest of my sins.

Already in the throes of a monumental deception, I blamed Guinevere for my fall from grace. For it was she, wasn't it, who was leading me down this unholy path?

I took a lantern with me in case I needed the extra light. Carrying the brass holder, I exited my suite. As I'd done once before, I crept past my parents' quarters and ventured toward the hallway that led to the Onyx Wing.

When I reached Mr. Wells's room, I stood outside his door, waiting to see if he sensed my presence.

Nothing happened. He didn't appear. He didn't lift me into his arms and whisk me off to his bed.

The burden of approaching him was mine.

Fear curled like smoke and drifted through my limbs, making me sway on my feet. Could I do this? Could I betray the duke after everything he'd done for me and my family? Or worse yet, could I give myself to a man outside the sanctity of matrimony?

To cure myself of my immoral ills, I made a prayerlike vow, promising to love, honor and obey Mr. Wells. In my heart, I made him my secret husband; in my heart, I became his one true wife.

On the heels of my fragile affiance, I turned his door handle and edged my way into the sitting room of his suite. With my breath held deeply in my lungs, I inched forward, preparing to enter the night-encompassed chamber where he slept.

~

Amber awakened in the middle of the night, aware that something was wrong. She reached out to connect with her lovers, and although Jay was crashed beside her, Luke's side of the bed was empty.

Troubled by his disappearance, she sat up and turned on a small nightlight. Jay didn't stir, but he was a sound sleeper. So was she, at least on most occasions.

How quickly she faltered. Already she was getting used to the weight of Luke's body and sounds of his breathing. Already she couldn't go back to sleep without him.

She glanced at the red digits on the alarm clock and climbed out of bed. Next, she grabbed a silk robe, warding off a two A.M. chill.

Determined to bring Luke back where he belonged, Amber considered his absence. Had he taken a side trip to the bathroom? No, she thought. He'd gone deliberately solo, seeking refuge in his own familiar space.

Protecting Jay's slumber, she darkened the room and went down the hall. Sure enough, she was right. A light shined beneath Luke's door.

She didn't knock. Instead she went inside, softly and quietly. Clad in only a pair of pajama bottoms, he was seated at his computer desk, tapping away at his keyboard. She moved closer, but he didn't appear to notice that she was there. His back was to her.

Although his room was cluttered, with discarded clothes and shelves of unevenly stacked books, she suspected that he had a handle on his masculine mess.

She took another step. Then, concerned about startling him, she alerted him to her presence. "Luke?"

His first reaction was to shrink the document on the screen, keeping his work private and making her feel like the intruder she was.

But she stayed anyway.

He turned around in his chair, and she tightened her robe.

Normally she would have loosened it, but a deep and aching sense of vulnerability had come over her.

"What are you doing up at this hour?" he asked.

"I can't sleep without you."

"Why? Because you've gotten used to having two men beside you?"

"Yes."

A frown furrowed his brow, and she realized it wasn't the answer he wanted to hear. But she'd spoken the truth, so she didn't retract it.

She changed the subject. "Are you working on the screenplay?"

He nodded.

"On the research or the story itself?"

"The story. But it's only a first draft. I'm still figuring things out."

"Like what?"

"Like how their relationship came to be."

Obviously he meant Curtis Wells and Lady Ellen. "What's to figure? They fucked each other silly. They got caught. He was killed, and she was sent away."

A bigger scowl appeared, marring his handsome features. "Cripes, Amber, where's your sense of romance?"

"I just don't see the appeal of a man who left his family behind."

"Are you talking about Curtis? Or your fathers?"

"All of them, I guess."

"According to the information I gathered, Curtis's ex-wife got remarried."

"And his daughter got a step-daddy. Well, hooray for her. I've had three step-daddies and look how I turned out."

Luke stood up, and she regretted her remarks. To stave him off, she held up her hand.

"Don't," she said.

"Don't what?"

"Start questioning me."

He didn't listen. "I want to know more about your childhood. More about the Amber who wanted a traditional wedding."

Damn it, she thought. Did his voice have to be so gentle? "That Amber is gone."

He scanned the length of her. Was he gauging her body language? Trying to decide how to proceed?

He said, "All right. I'll let it go for now. But we are going to talk about it sometime."

He'd missed his calling, she thought. He was good at psychobabble. But she supposed that was what made him care about Curtis and Lady Ellen, what made him interested in figuring them out.

"Tell me about your screenplay, Luke."

He sat on the edge of his bed, inviting her to join him. "What do you want to know about it?"

She took a spot next to him, and the closeness made her feel vulnerable again. But she did her best to seem relaxed. "Tell me how you think their relationship came to be."

"Truthfully? I think he charmed her in the beginning, but later, I think she seduced him."

"Really? You think she initiated sex the first time? Why?"

"Because I don't think Curtis would've gone after her in that way, not with her being engaged to the duke. He would've wanted to, but he would've held back."

"So you're laying the blame on her?"

"I'm not blaming anyone. It's just how I see it."

"And how you're going to write it?"

"Yes."

"Maybe I'm more like Lady Ellen than I thought."

"Because you seduced Jay and me the first time? Because you're still seducing us?" He looked into her eyes. "You've become like her to me."

"You seem like him to me, too." And he had from the beginning. Nothing had changed in that regard.

"Good, because when I sell the screenplay and get the movie made, I intend to play his part."

Her heart went jittery. He seemed confident that it was

going to sell, but he was probably right. She could see it happening for him. His breakout project. His claim to success.

"Will you take me to the premiere?" she asked, part joking, part serious, part confused. Did she want to walk the red carpet with him? Did she want to sit in a darkened theater and watch her great-great-grandfather's life unfold on the screen with her lover playing the part?

"You know I'd take you," he said. "But that's a ways off."

Maybe they wouldn't even be lovers by then, she thought. Or friends. Or anything. Especially if Amber walked away like she normally did. "No point in jumping the gun."

"No. No point." He stood up. "I'm going to go back to work. But you can stay if you want."

"Stay?"

"Here in my room. You can curl up in my bed."

Until when? He got tired and joined her? "I don't think I should." She was already struggling with her attachment to him.

His chest rose and fell, indicating that his breathing had gone rough. "Why not?"

"Because you're supposed to be staying in the other room with me and Jay."

"I can't. Not tonight."

She glanced at his computer. The screen saver had turned

the monitor dark. "You might be like Curtis, but you'd never do what he did."

He misunderstood. "Die for someone?"

"No. Leave your wife and child behind."

"That's true. But he should have met Lady Ellen first. He should have made a life with her."

"Some things aren't meant to be."

He didn't respond, creating a gap in their conversation. But there were other gaps, too. Amber was still seated on the edge of his bed. A part of her didn't want to leave, the part that was like Lady Ellen, she supposed.

"Where do you think it happened?" she asked. "Where do you think they first made love?"

"I don't know. Outdoors, maybe. Or it could've been in Curtis's room. I could picture Lady Ellen going to him in the middle of the night."

"The way I just showed up in your room?"

He shook his head. "You came here to bring me back to you and another man. It isn't the same."

"It's still me wanting you."

"Not the way she wanted him."

"Sex is sex."

"What they had was more than sex."

She finally stood up, needing to distance herself from his bed. "What are you saying? That you want me to love you?"

"No. *No.*" He got defensive. "That's Jay's game. Trying to trick us into thinking we're in love."

"Then what's yours?"

"Mine isn't a game."

"We're all playing a game, Luke. It's all a masquerade."

"I just want to be alone with you."

"And I promised that we would be. After the wedding night, we'll go on a date. We'll get naked. We'll do everything a couple should do together." Because the thought scared her, she twisted the tie on her robe.

"Yeah, and I can see how much it thrills you."

More fear. More confusion. "It would be easier if you weren't so possessive."

"Who said it was supposed to be easy?"

He walked toward her and he kept walking until she got so scattered, she backed herself into a corner. He'd set the ultimate trap, pinning her against the wall. In a battle of wills, they stared at each other.

Fighting her emotions, she said, "Don't you dare kiss me." Not now, not while she was out of her element, not while she felt like a caged bird.

He leaned over and put his mouth against the pulse at her neck, nipping her instead.

She caught her breath, but it didn't deter him. If anything, it only fueled his fire. He grabbed the tie on her robe and undid it, pulling the silk garment open and leaving her bare to his touch.

Like the frustrated man he was, he pushed his body closer to hers. As his burgeoning cock nudged the softness between her legs, she waited to see what he would do next.

Would he try to fuck her? Shoved up against a wall?

No, she thought. Not Luke. Not for their first time alone. He was too gentlemanly for that.

"I'm sorry," he said, and let her go.

"I know." But knowing didn't make their relationship any less tangled.

"Go back to Jay," he told her.

Yes, she thought, back to safety. Back to the man who understood their ménage.

~

Was Mr. Wells my groom? Was I truly his bride? Or had I merely created a farce in my mind?

The door to his chamber was closed, and I'd yet to open it. I remained in the sitting room, contemplating my actions.

I wanted him, Heaven help me I did. But was I doing the right thing?

Whatever the answer, my need was too great to turn back. My only recourse was to move forward, to take a heartfelt chance, no matter what the eventual outcome.

Holding to that thought, I opened his bedchamber door, slowly, cautiously, and it creaked softly from my effort.

The low-burning lantern in my hand cast a small ray of light in an otherwise pitch-dark room. I lifted it a tad higher, scanning the interior.

The bed was rumpled, the heavy brocade quilt and satin sheets bunched. I looked closer and realized that it was empty, that there was no strong, swarthy man heaped within its finery.

Where, pray tell, was Mr. Wells? Had he gone for a midnight walk? Was he in the garden, strolling solemnly amongst the roses? Or was he exploring the moonlit shore and gazing out at the sea?

Confused, I placed the lantern on his nightstand, wondering what I should do. Should I slip outside and search for him? Or should I crawl into his bed and wait for his return?

Just then, I heard a familiar voice emerge from the corner behind me. "What are you doing here, Lady Ellen?"

"I'm here to see you."

"See me?"

"Be with you." I wanted to turn around, but I was too nervous to meet his gaze. I surmised that he'd heard someone enter his suite and had gotten out of bed to investigate. Taking to the shadows, he'd discovered the person invading his privacy was me.

"Are you certain this is what you want?" he asked.

"Yes." Fearful as I was, I'd never been more certain of anything. I could hear him moving closer. Soon his arms would encircle my waist and his breath would flutter across my nape.

"The guilt will be ours to share," he said, acknowledging our wrongdoing. "But, damn, you tempt me so."

Would it ease his conscience if I told him about the vow I'd made? Or would being a husband again, even a make-believe one, only heighten his burden?

Needless to say, I kept quiet. My secret wouldn't absolve us.

As predicted, he pressed the front of his body to the back of mine and slipped his arms around me. When he buried his face against my neck, I knew he was drinking me in.

"Are you bare beneath your dressing gown?" he asked.

Unable to find my voice, I nodded.

He undid the tie and the luxurious garment fluttered open. "You're wicked. More wicked than I am."

I forced myself to speak. "That isn't possible." By now, he was caressing my breasts and running his thumbs over my nipples, making me ache for more. "What you're doing to me."

"Likewise, my lady." He bumped my bottom with his arousal and made me gasp. I could feel him through his drawers, and he was as hard as a wand from a hawthorn tree.

He continued his quest, sliding his hands lower. He skimmed my navel, and my stomach muscles quavered beneath his thrilling touch.

"*The clandestine goddess*," he said.

The carnal knight, I thought. He put his fingers against my most private place, igniting a fire between my watery legs.

I leaned back against him, using the wall of his chest for support. He was making salacious little circles, pleasing me the way I'd pleased myself in the bathtub, only it was naughtier coming from him. He held me open with one hand and strummed me with the other.

Not being able to see him intensified the mystery, the forbidden allure. I turned my head, and he nuzzled my cheek, making me lustfully dreamy in his arms.

He was magic, I thought. *Light magic. Dark magic.* Somewhere during his spell, I had become his sexual servant. There was nothing I wouldn't allow him to do to me, nothing I wouldn't do for him.

Caught in the throes of my hunger, I climaxed, wet and shuddering, hot and dizzy. If I hadn't been braced against him, I would have fallen to the ground.

A fainted lady. A clay virgin in his hands.

"Say my name," he implored me. "My given name."

"Curtis," I whispered. *My Curtis.*

He removed my robe, and it slid from my body, pooling at my feet. Kicking it aside, he scooped me up and carried me to his bed.

CHAPTER TEN

Once we were in bed, he didn't remove his nightshirt or drawers. He simply leaned over me, bracing the bulk of his weight
upon his arms.

"Curtis," I said, repeating his name. I could have said it a
thousand times.

"Ellen," he responded, making the moment even more intimate. He was the first nonfamilial man who'd ever addressed
me without my title.

He lowered his head to kiss me, and I succumbed to his
magic, to the dream he incited. As our tongues tangled, as our
worlds collided, I pictured us running away together, so far
and so fast, we disappeared into a mist.

I moaned softly, and he dropped down on top of me, pressing his body against mine. He was erect beneath his drawers, and the blatant hardness caused me to catch my breath.

When the kissing paused, I said, "I want to touch you." To learn to caress him.

"You will. But not until I taste you."

I touched a finger to my lips. "You were tasting me."

"Down there, my lady."

He'd gone formal again, but nonetheless, he made me blush. My bathtub foray came to mind: how I sloshed back and forth in the water, imagining his tongue inside me.

I nodded, giving him permission, and he made a roughly aroused sound. Beside us, the candle on the nightstand flickered.

He slid down my body, nuzzling my bared flesh along the way. When he stopped at my navel, I ached from the want of him.

He glanced up, making certain that I was watching. I was. Oh, how I was. But I fought bouts of shyness, too.

"It's all right," he said against my stomach.

My entire body quavered. He was my knight. My Lancelot. "It just seems so forbidden."

"Like us?"

"Yes." I reached out to tame his hair, to move a strand away from his eyes, where it had fallen in unruly disarray.

"Open your legs."

My cheeks turned hot, but I did his bidding, spreading myself for him. Instinctively, I lifted my bottom, as well.

He smiled, quite devilishly. "You want this as badly as I do."

He was right. I very much did. As he moved lower, my senses heightened. The smell of burning wax drifted to my nostrils, and nocturnal sights and sounds permeated my mind.

Curtis lifted my legs onto his shoulders, and I grappled with the sheets, struggling to clutch whatever I could. But it was to no avail; the material slid away from me.

Soft and slow, he placed his lips against me, and I bucked like a wild mare. One sweet kiss, and I wanted to rub myself all over him.

"Shhh." He tried to calm me, but he wasn't the one being tortured.

I battled the linens again. What else could I do? He took his time, teasing me with small, playful licks. Up and down he went, all along my slit, and with each flick of his tongue, I got wetter and wetter.

"Next time you can sit directly on my face," he said.

Next time? Oh, mercy. Oh, heaven's gate. I could barely sustain the wicked pleasure from this time.

He was toying with the tiny nub that would create my climax. Possessive, I tunneled my hands through his hair, tugging him closer.

"Don't ever do this to any one else," I told him.

"You would deny me other lovers? Even when we are no longer?"

"Yes." I couldn't bear for him to make anyone else feel this way. I wanted the insanity reserved for me.

He didn't respond, but he laved me harder. He even sucked on the nub with which he'd been toying, making my pulse pound at that very spot.

I rocked against him, needing to fuel the lust-driven flame. Kindling spirits, I thought, steeped in blood-soaring heat.

He clutched my bottom so strongly, I wondered if by the time he was done, his handprints would be branded upon my skin.

The scent of wax got heavier, and so did the air in my lungs. He continued his blissful torture, devouring me like nectar from the gods.

Carnal moisture coated his lips. I could even hear him swallowing it. Nothing had ever seemed so lewd, so lustfully unchaste until he looked up at me and said that he loved my cunt.

I gasped at the vulgarity of the word he'd chosen. Yet in my orgasmic stage, I got horribly, terribly excited. I liked that he'd said something dirty.

He might be my knight, but he was still a gunsmith, a wild American sowing his Glenmoor oats. Few men would've dared to speak to a lady that way.

Unable to stop myself, I climaxed against his probing tongue. I tugged once again at his hair, thrilled when he sipped more and more of my juices.

I shook; I shivered; I suppressed the noises that rose in the back of my throat, afraid I would wake the entire estate.

In the aftermath, he wiped his mouth and slid my legs from his shoulders.

I didn't know what to do, so I remained quiet, lost in the nearness of him.

He removed his nightshirt and tossed it onto the other side of the bed. As he peeled off his drawers, I watched and waited.

His phallus sprang free, and I gazed at the thick, hardened length and the pearl-tipped crown. Although I had an idea of how an erect penis would look, I hadn't envisioned the ruddy color or purplish veins.

"You made me leak," he said.

Fascinated by the sheer maleness of him, I continued to stare. "I didn't mean to."

"You can touch it now."

I reached down, hoping my hand didn't shake. Suddenly I was nervous again. "Show me what to do."

"This." He covered my hand with his and curled his fingers around mine, helping me grip the base of his shaft. "And this." He moved our joined hands.

Soon I was milking him, moving up and down. He was hard yet silky, and I liked the sensation. Touching him made my stomach flutter. He seemed to be having the same reaction. His muscles were jumping.

"Is this all right?" I asked, smearing the moisture at the crown and caressing him with it.

"That's more than all right." His eyes had gone dark, nearly as black as the night. I was holding his power in my hands.

Curious, I cupped his testes and realized how truly fragile they were. I almost nicked him with a fingernail.

"Women like you are dangerous," he said.

Innocent ladies? Proper ladies? I trailed upward again, back to the tiny slit at the tip, back to another bead of moisture.

"I wonder," I said, musing more to myself than to him, "what it tastes like."

A light came back to his eyes, a shimmer from the candle. "You can't put your mouth there."

"Why not?" All I was going to do was take one dainty lick.

"Because you can't. Not this time. I'm too . . ."

He nudged me down, and my playtime was over. He was ready to copulate, to take my virginity, to fill me with his seed.

With a burst of excitement, of fear, I released the air in my lungs and waited.

But he stopped and reached for his nightshirt, tucking it carefully beneath me. Puzzled, I only gazed at him.

"To absorb the maiden's blood," he said, making certain that it didn't stain the sheets.

The evidence of our sin, I thought, of me behaving like his bride.

Amber chose a hillside bungalow at the Chateau Marmont for the masquerade. Wonderfully swank and wildly dramatic, the hotel had boasted a decadent reputation since the 1930s. Even the ghosts that haunted it were said to be naughty.

And no wonder. A lush hideaway above the Sunset Strip, the Chateau Marmont was the place to misbehave. Supposedly this was where Clark Gable and Jean Harlow had done the nasty while she'd been on her honeymoon with another man. That alone made it one of Amber's favorite hotels and the seemingly right location for the offbeat wedding night she'd planned.

So here she was, alone in the bungalow, anticipating the most thrilling threesome of her life. The wildest sex game she'd ever played.

She could've brought in someone to do her hair and makeup, but she'd decided that she wanted this moment to be private. True, she'd hired a team of professionals to turn Jay and Luke into the same man, but that was different. Amber would be looking like herself. She didn't need assistance for that.

Because it was still early, she hadn't gotten ready yet. Instead, she wandered the floor plan, which included a spacious living room, fireplace, full kitchen and dining area. Accommodations at the Chateau Marmont were individually decorated, and this bungalow showcased lavish antiques with a bohemian flair.

There were two bedrooms. The master, of course, would serve as the room with the marriage bed. The other would be her dressing room. Already her gown was hanging on a peg attached to a triple-mirrored armoire.

She reached out and touched the satin sheath. She'd had it created for this occasion, but that was easy for her. With her trust fund wealth and high fashion connections, she had the resources to obtain a fantasy gown and do it within a matter of days.

Not that anyone who'd been involved in making the dress would think that she was marrying for real. Amber was known for attending masquerades, and she'd told her peers that it was being used as a costume. As for the intimate details, she didn't care what other people thought. All that mattered were the principal players.

She hadn't gone with Jay and Luke to pick out the sex toys. She'd decided to let them surprise her.

The men's suitcases were already here, making it easier for them to arrive unburdened. Although they'd packed toiletries and a change of clothes for the next day, they hadn't included the toys. Amber would have to wait to see those.

Would they bring big, blasting dildos? God, she hoped so.

To glamorize the erotic theme and provide the food and drink of choice, she'd ordered a lusciously decorated cake and a bottle of vintage champagne that would be delivered closer to the event.

Impatient, she glanced at her diamond-encrusted watch. Too much time to kill. The sun had only begun to set.

Needing a breath of fresh air, she walked outside to view the private garden. Instantly, she noticed a row of neatly trimmed rosebushes, and red was the primary color.

Would Luke think she'd requested this specific garden? She hadn't. And now that she'd seen it, she was uncomfortably transfixed. A stroke of fate had provided the type of flowers she'd been trying to avoid.

Amber turned away from the roses. She'd come here for a wedding-night ménage, and, by damn, that was what was going to happen.

She returned to the bungalow, thinking about her lovers. By now, they would be in the midst of their transformation, becoming two identical husbands.

For one anxious bride.

～

Luke sat next to Jay in front of lighted mirrors. The makeup lab belonged to Harley McCoy, a friend of Amber's, who was also a freelance special effects artist.

He and his team had gone to Santa Fe and created their movie-style magic on Luke and Jay for the first masquerade, and now they were doing it again.

A few changes had been made, refining the makeup to accommodate their own features, rather than the man they'd impersonated last time. Regardless, they were looking more and more like each other.

Naturally, their entire bodies had been spray tanned, altering their skin tones to give them the same complexion. Since both of them normally kept their chests free of hair, that area had been untouched. But to maximize the effect, their pubic regions had been dyed darker and trimmed in the exact manner.

As for the hair on their heads, soon they would be fitted with jet black wigs, cut in a contemporary style and combed straight back. Their soft, form-fitting masks were black, too, obscuring the tops of their faces and bridges of their noses, leaving their nostrils, mouths and jawlines exposed.

Costume-wise, they would be wearing Armani tuxedoes with satin shirts the same oyster color as Amber's dress.

Jay glanced over and grinned. Luke only rolled his eyes. He wished he was as eager as his roommate, but Luke wasn't trying to dismiss a previous marriage. Farce or not, this would be his first wedding.

"Quit being such a pisser," Jay said.

"I'm not," Luke shot back.

"If you ruin this for Amber, she's going to be mad."

"I already promised her that I wouldn't." He'd given his word that he wouldn't do or say anything that would deliberately give himself away. He'd vowed to protect his and Jay's identities.

They fell silent, and hours later their masquerade was complete—makeup, costumes and all.

Harley praised himself and his team. "Your own mothers wouldn't know you," he said to the grooms. "In fact, I don't even know who's who anymore."

"I'm the sexy one," Jay responded, using the Southern accent they'd perfected last time.

"Funny guy," Luke said in the same tone. It wasn't as slow and deep-drawled as his natural voice, but it came easily to him. He knew Jay had to work harder at it.

Harley chuckled. He was a robust man with a pointed goatee. "You boys better get going."

They went outside where night had fallen and a long, sleek limousine waited. Amber had taken care of everything. Except the toys, Luke thought. Both he and Jay had created a bag of tricks for their bride's pleasure.

Jay climbed into the back of the car, and Luke sat across from him.

Soon they were on their way. As always, his roommate leaned back and relaxed, leaving his goodie bag on the seat beside him. Not Luke. He sat forward, clutching the drawstring on his.

"I think she's going to like what we cooked up," Jay said.

"Yeah, I'm sure she will."

"It's okay for you to like it, too."

Luke shook his head, and they both laughed. This entire scenario was absurd. But as much as Luke hated to admit it, it was oddly sexy, too. He knew the minute he saw Amber he was going to get a raging hard-on.

The limo traveled along Sunset, getting closer to the hotel. When they arrived, the driver took them directly to the bungalow Amber had rented.

"Showtime," Jay said.

Luke nodded. His heart wouldn't quit pounding. His cock was already stirring, too.

When he blew out a laden breath, his sidekick asked, "You okay, bro?"

"I'm fine." Just nervous about pretending to become a husband, he thought. He'd been imagining her in the wedding dress she'd described, and now the moment was here.

The chauffeur opened the car door and Luke got out first. Jay made his exit, and they tipped the driver.

Once the limo disappeared into the Hollywood night, they took the walkway to the bungalow.

"We really do look alike," Jay said, his masked face catching a ray of moonlight.

"I still think she'll know the difference."

"Why? Because of the connection you have with her?"

"I never said I had a connection with her."

Jay ignored Luke's denial and gestured to the softly sheered windows on the bungalow. "She has the lights down low."

"I don't think the semi-darkness will help."

"You just want her to recognize you. To feel your aura or whatever."

"I don't want anything but to get this over with."

"If you say so." As Jay switched to the accent, he prepared to use the front door key that had been provided.

Luke's heart started pounding again. But he tempered his emotions and got into character, becoming the same man as Jay.

His roommate opened the door, and they went inside. Amber was nowhere to be found, but the scene had been romantically set. In addition to the dimmed lights, votive candles burned throughout the bungalow. She'd promised to create a beautiful environment, and she had.

Regardless, Luke reminded himself that it was only a game, especially when he glanced at the dining area.

The table featured a frothy wedding cake, artfully decorated and topped with a brunette bride and two masked grooms. The iced champagne was a 1996 Fleury Brut.

"Where do you think she is?" Jay asked.

"I don't know," Luke responded.

Just then, her long, flowing reflection appeared on the other side of a glass door that led to a patio. No, Luke, thought. A garden. He could see a haze of flowers in the distance.

She opened the door, and as she crossed the threshold, silence engulfed the room.

Her sleek satin gown clung elegantly to her curves, the pleated train gathered in back. Around her neck was a single strand of pearls, and her cosmetic application was softly muted yet wildly sensual. She glowed in all the right places. At her ears were a set of sapphires drops, enhancing the bluish green of her eyes. Her angular bob, free of adornment, had been styled to silken perfection.

Luke wanted to pull her into his arms and kiss her. Jay probably did, too.

"You're here," she said, gazing from one man to the other.

She sounded nervous, sweetly anxious, making the charade seem real.

Yet there was no recognition in her eyes. But it was still early, Luke thought.

Leaving plenty of time for her to identify them.

CHAPTER ELEVEN

"You're absolutely gorgeous," one of the grooms said.

"Thank you." Amber studied him, then turned to analyze the other masked man. Thankfully, she didn't have a clue as to who was who. They were mirror images of each other.

Would she know once she kissed them? Once they put their wondrous hands on her? She prayed that she never figured it out. Already she'd spent too much time in the garden, obsessing about Luke.

"You're handsome." She fingered the pearls at her neck. "Both of you." Tall and dark and mysterious.

"Glad you think so," the same groom said.

"That's quite a cake," the other one remarked, using an identical accent.

"We can eat it after the vows." She wanted to take turns feeding them and having them feed her. Creamy bites, sensual nibbles. The sweetly frothed, custard-filled confection was a delight she'd been waiting for.

"Yes, the vows," he said. "Do you have them memorized?"

"Yes." They'd agreed on simple, sexy words. "I'm going to promise to honor and obey you in bed."

"Yes, you are."

Was he Jay or was he Luke? Whoever he was, he was making her uncomfortable. In her mind, she named him Groom A as a means to identify him. For now, Groom B was being quiet.

Groom A shifted the velvet bag in his hand.

She worried that he was Luke, especially since Luke had a type A personality and Jay was a type B.

Had she named them appropriately?

She glanced at Groom B, but he didn't react. What did she expect? For him to behave like Jay? Both men knew better than to spoil this for her.

"We need to get started," A said.

"Yes, we do," B added. "Right now." He'd become aggressive, too, as determined as his counterpart.

Now she was thoroughly confused. But that was the point, wasn't it? To keep her guessing.

"We have a surprise for you," A said. "Something to go along with the vows."

Each of them took one of her hands and led her to the master bedroom. Excitement mingled with fear. Exactly what type of surprise did they have in mind?

Once inside the candle-laced room, they dumped the contents of their black bags onto the bed. A colorful array of dildos, glass wands, vibrators, creams, lubricants and oils spilled out.

Before she had time to comment on the items they'd provided, Groom A reached into his jacket pocket and produced a luxurious blindfold. Amber flinched. She'd never relinquished that kind of control, not to anyone.

"You can't use that," she said, no matter how pretty it would look with her gown.

Groom A persisted. "It'll only be for a few seconds."

"Seconds?" She slanted him a wary look. "Nothing could be that quick."

"He means minutes," Groom B clarified and gentled his voice. The softer tone made him seem like Luke.

Talk about tricking her. They were good, she thought, damned good at their roles. She divided her gaze between them. "Does the blindfold have to be part of the vows?"

"We think it does," A responded.

"What for?" she asked.

"For the mystery," he answered again. "Don't you want us to tease you? To thrill you?"

Of course she did. By now, every bone in her body was turning to mush. "I don't like having my eyes covered."

"We won't hurt you." This from Groom B. "We just want to make you our wife."

Their wife.

That was what she wanted, too. But just for tonight, she reminded herself, just for the game. "Okay." Her breath rushed out. "You can use the blindfold."

"Good girl," they said in unison, then laughed at their natural ability to mimic each other, adding another twin twist to the charade.

A beat of silence passed, and her heart thumped, making her more aware of her nervousness.

Groom A nudged her to her knees and put the blindfold around her eyes. Everything went pitch-dark. She could feel the presence of her soon-to-be husbands, and she could smell the candles burning, but she couldn't see her fate.

She heard both men moving about the room. Then she realized that one of them had come back and was standing in front of her. But which one?

"Ready?" he asked, his voice undetectable.

She smoothed the waistband of her gown. She could feel the train bunched up on the floor behind her. "Yes."

"Do you promise to honor and obey us? To be our nasty little wife? To come when we want you to come?"

It seemed strange to be down on her knees, becoming an erotic bride. Strange, but exciting. The ultimate masquerade.

"Yes," she said. "I promise."

He slipped something into her hand, and she clutched the large, circular item. It was cool and hard. Stainless steel, she thought, with a hole in the center and engraving around it.

"It's a penis ring," he said.

Her heart hit her chest. "To seal the vow?"

"Exactly." The rasp of his zipper sounded.

Heaven help her. He was freeing his cock. "May I remove the blindfold now?"

"No."

He was going to make her fit the ring into place without using her sight? "What if I—?"

"Don't worry. I'll help you."

She waited in the dark and he moved closer, guiding her to his semi-erect penis. No doubt she would be doing this for her other groom, too.

Amber wasn't a cock ring expert, but she knew the typical way to wear them was around the base of the shaft and the balls. The purpose was to restrict blood flow and prolong an erection. But this was more than that.

She was marrying him.

Together, they made it happen. She held the ring, and he maneuvered his package. He dropped one testicle through, then the other. While he was pushing his penis through, her clit tingled. Her grooms were nasty boys.

"All done." He bumped the tip against her lips, letting her know that he wanted her to kiss it.

She decided to give him more than that. She licked the head, swirling her tongue and teasing him with her blowjob skills. He cupped her face, inspiring her to pleasure him all the way.

While she sucked, while he got more and more aroused, she tried to figure out who he was. It wasn't supposed to matter; she wasn't supposed to care, but somewhere deep inside, she did.

The way he thrust his hips, the way he took possession, the way he pushed toward the back of her throat . . .

He felt like Luke.

If only she could look up and see him, if only she could confirm if he was A or B.

Clutching her scalp, he made rough sounds.

Amber squeezed her thighs together. She was getting wet. She loved her naughty wedding. And she loved the cock in her mouth.

Luke's cock?

"Damn," she heard the other groom say. Obviously he was watching, hoping he would get the same lusty treatment.

Heightening the game, she sucked deeper. She wanted to please both of them.

The man getting the blowjob whispered her name, and she reached out to caress the ring around his shaft and balls.

Was he Luke?

Hot and sexy, he flared against her tongue. When he shivered, when he went into a full-body shake, she reveled in the excitement of being a new bride. The cock ring gave him extra staying power, but he was still fighting it. She was making him desperate, eager, crazy to come.

He seemed like Luke. So much like Luke.

She tried to clear her mind, but she thought about the screenplay and the roses and every other thing that reminded her of him.

Behind the blindfold, she was consumed with him. By now, she knew he was Luke. She couldn't say how she knew, other than a familiar feeling, an emotion, an erotic intuition.

Amber should have cursed her knowledge, and she probably would later. But at the moment, she couldn't stop what she knew.

She couldn't stop his ejaculation, either. Lost in the act, he spilled warm and wet into her mouth, and she swallowed every milky drop.

He stepped back afterward, and the other groom—Jay—

came forward. But he didn't repeat the process, at least not right away. He gave her time to recuperate.

Finally, when he produced a cock ring, she married him just as willingly as she'd married Luke. She gave him oral sex, too. She did everything exactly the same, only it wasn't the same. No matter how clever their charade, no matter if they were masked or if she was blindfolded, they were two different men, and they made her feel two different ways.

Finally, her blindfold was removed. She squinted, adjusting to the candlelight, and got to her feet.

The men gave her their rings and recited their vows, playing their husbandly parts. She studied both objects and noticed how ornate the engraving on them was, very much like wedding bands. She placed them on the dresser.

She glanced up and made eye contact with Luke, and as their gazes locked, another bout of clarity slammed into her brain. Suddenly she knew that he was Groom B, not A, as she'd originally thought.

Groom B. The one who'd told her how absolutely gorgeous she was in her wedding dress, the one who'd first softened his voice, who'd been gentler, more romantic.

"I know who's who," she blurted, rather than keep her turmoil to herself.

"You could be confused," A said.

"I'm not. You're Jay."

He didn't confirm or deny her allegation. He gestured to his twin. "Are you sure he's Luke?"

"Yes."

"How can you be certain?"

"I just can." She wasn't comfortable explaining that she could feel the difference.

Jay spoke again, still using the accent, still trying to trick her. "Be funny if you were wrong."

"I'm not." She'd been telling herself all along that who was who didn't matter, that she would block their identities in her mind if she had to. But she couldn't, not completely.

She looked at Luke once again, but he didn't join the conversation. He didn't do anything. He just stood very still.

Jay took her hand. "Maybe we should have some cake and champagne now." He, too, looked at his roommate. "All of us."

Yes, Amber thought, all of them. She reached out to Luke, offering him her other hand. Regardless of her knowledge, this was still a ménage.

And it was still her wedding night.

～

Luke moved forward, accepting Amber's invitation and completing the circle. The strange circle, he thought, that had become an even stranger bond.

He'd wanted Amber to figure out who he was, but now

that she had, he wished she hadn't, making him more confused than ever. Was it because it made their relationship seem too real? Too attached?

He didn't know what to think, other than life had a way of throwing curveballs, and baseball had never been his game.

"Let's go," Jay said, remaining in character and prodding the trio into the living room.

Luke stayed in character, too.

Amber was holding tightly to his hand, but she was holding onto Jay just as firmly. Luke assumed it was her way of treating them as equal grooms.

Once they were gathered around the table, Luke offered to open the champagne, which had been chilling in a silver ice bucket.

"Hell of a vintage." He complimented Amber on her taste. He popped the cork and poured everyone a glass.

They raised their flutes, and she made a threesome toast. "To my husbands."

"Which one of these guys is supposed to be me?" Jay wobbled the grooms on the cake. "Oh, wait. They're the same, aren't they?"

"You can take your pick," Amber told him.

"Then I'll be him." He tapped the figure of his choice, then turned to Luke, stating the obvious. "That makes you the other guy."

"The one standing to the right of the bride?" Luke gave him a suspicious look.

Amber sipped her champagne. "Don't snipe about it. We already established that they're the same."

Luke disagreed. "A real groom normally stands to the right of the bride." And he didn't trust that Jay hadn't given him that spot purposefully.

Amber dipped into the cake and scooped a glob of icing onto her finger. "Where a *real* groom stands doesn't matter. We're just pretending." She sucked her finger clean, then made a curious face. "I wonder why that became the tradition."

"I know why," Jay said.

"So do I," Luke shot back.

"Then tell her."

"Fine, I will." He shifted his full attention to Amber. "In the old days, the right arm was considered the arm of the sword. So if a man had to protect his bride, he would hold her with his left hand and fight off attackers with his right arm."

"Oh, that's nice. It makes a groom seem like a knight." She angled her head. "How did you know that?"

He met her gaze, feeling a bit knightly himself. By now he was speaking in his natural voice. "From my sisters." He motioned to Jay. "And he probably knew because he's been married before."

Trancelike, Amber only nodded. Suddenly she seemed dreamy and romantic. Almost like a real bride.

Also using his natural voice, Jay said, "Now that we've totally blown our roles, should we remove our masks, too?"

Amber snapped out of her trance. "No."

"You still want us to look the same, even if we're being ourselves now?"

"Yes, please."

"Please." Jay smiled, slipping back into the honeymoon. "That's sweet. Our wife has manners."

She swatted his arm, and they both laughed. Luke envied his roommate that. He was good at easing tension. Luke, on the other hand, had the penchant for creating it.

"I'll cut the cake." Jay wielded the ribbon-wrapped knife that was on the table.

The three of them were standing beside the frothy delicacy, the way a bride and groom would be at a wedding.

"Will you feed me a bite?" Amber asked Jay.

"Of course I will," he responded.

"You, too?" she asked Luke.

"Yes, me, too." Fulfilling her fantasies was what he and Jay had initially agreed to do.

The other man sliced a big piece of cake and slid it onto a plate for everyone to share.

"Since you got to marry her first," Jay said, "I get to feed her first."

Yeah, Luke thought. He'd married her first. He'd even been depicted as the groom on the right. The knight. He was still reeling from the feeling.

Jay broke off a small bite and brought it to Amber's mouth. While she ate it, she licked the icing from her lips.

Luke's cock went stiff, and he damned his attraction to her. She'd already made him come. That should've been enough to keep him from getting hard again. But nothing was ever enough, not when it came to Amber.

He was anxious for his turn. But Jay was taking his time, offering her more cake and encouraging her to suck on his fingers.

It was almost surreal to watch them because they really looked like a bride and groom. But then, why wouldn't they? They were dressed for the occasion.

The ritual continued, with Amber feeding Jay playful bites and kissing him after each one. Tongue to tongue they connected, and the process was lustfully messy.

When she broke off another bite of cake and turned to Luke, his heart hit his chest. No more waiting.

As she held it out to him, crumbs dropped onto the floor. "It has lemon custard inside."

She popped the dessert into his mouth, and he almost moaned. The custard was sweet and tangy, but what came next was even better. She kissed him just seconds after he swallowed the treat.

Now he wanted to peel off her dress and do cake-obsessed things to her. Trapped in the throes of getting harder, he grasped her hips, bumping her with his fly.

"I think Luke likes being married," he heard Jay say.

"Do you?" Amber asked.

He tugged her closer. "Yes."

"We're only playing," she reminded him.

"Then I want to play some more."

"With the toys?"

"With the cake."

She smiled. "In what way?"

"With your dress off."

"You'll have to help get me out of it." She glanced over at the other man. "Both of you."

Jay didn't hesitate. He came up behind her, preparing to unzip her gown.

Together, they stripped her down to her lingerie, and Luke stepped back to admire her. She wore a naughty ensemble of white lace that included an old-fashioned corset, thigh-high stockings, and crotchless panties.

"These are hot." Jay toyed with the panties.

Luke couldn't agree more. "They're perfect." Especially for what he had in mind.

He approached the cake and gave the bride and her grooms a slight push, making them tumble in a sexy heap.

From there, he gathered a stream of icing onto his finger and rubbed it against Amber's clit, giving her a sweet, sweet shiver. A dollop of custard came next, making her breath catch.

While Jay watched, Luke got on his knees to enjoy the experience.

Whether he was actually married or not.

CHAPTER TWELVE

I wasn't Curtis's bride, but as I lay there, looking up at him, I was fooled into believing that I was.

He'd yet to enter me, and I was anticipating our joining.

He lowered his head to kiss me, softly, slowly, in the most romantic of ways. The hardness of his body weighed beautifully upon mine.

But still, he didn't enter me.

I waited, my heart centered on him. He ended the kiss, and our gazes locked.

"I don't want to hurt you," he said.

I relied on what I assumed was scientific knowledge. "The pain will subside."

"*Will it?*" *He wasn't talking about me losing my maiden-head. He was referring to something much, much deeper.*

"*I don't want to think about that,*" *I told him. I wanted to keep pretending that I was his bride.*

"*Nor do I. But I can't seem to help it. You shouldn't have come to me, Ellen.*"

My heart, still centered on him, began to ache. "*Then send me away.*"

"*Now?*" *He steadied his breath, his body, his troubled spirit.* "*If only I could.*"

He kissed me again, and suddenly I was afraid of being hurt, of missing him for the rest of my forsaken life.

When his tongue slipped past my lips, I put my arms around him. He nudged my legs apart and reached down, fitting himself against me. The crown of his penis pushed at my opening, and I gripped his shoulders.

He went in, part way, stretching me. Nothing had ever felt so right yet so wrong. The intimacy was almost more than I could bear.

He nuzzled my ear. "*Are you all right?*"

Not trusting myself to speak, I nodded. I was trying not to tense, but I knew what was coming.

"*Don't cry out.*" *He was warning me, bracing me for deeper penetration, for a quick thrust.*

I recovered my voice, soft as it was. "*I won't.*"

Heaven! Oh, mercy! He impaled me all the way, and it hurt so desperately, I bit my lip. At the same time he'd torn my maidenhead, I tasted my own blood.

He stopped and looked down at me. In the silence, he licked the crimson from my lips, tasting it for himself and making me aware of how primal he was. A rough gentleman, I thought, an enigma.

He moved inside me, slower this time, creating gentle friction. The rhythm affected me like a sweet, choppy wave. It still hurt, but it felt mystifyingly good, too.

I smiled at him, and he returned the gesture with a grin.

"You like my cock," he said, teasing me.

My cheeks went hot. He was clever with those dirty words, wild Texan that he was.

I gazed at where we were joined. We looked good together, even there. His pubis was dark, where mine was fair, and his penis—his cock—went in and out. As for his testes, they were drawn tight.

"Most women don't watch," he said.

"Am I being too bold?"

"God, no." His expression was intense now, his forehead grooved in lines of sensual concentration. "It arouses me. You arouse me."

I kept watching, and Curtis angled his hips so I could get a clearer view. His nightshirt was still positioned beneath me, the fabric rubbing against my bottom as he rocked back and forth. Slow, then fast, then slow again.

"I'm not going to spill into you," he said.

I glanced up. I'd been expecting the warmth of his seed, which was foolish of me. At least he knew better. But he'd already fathered a child.

"Then where?" I asked.

"I'll do it here." He trailed a finger down my stomach, circling my navel, making my flesh tingle. "And I'll clean you when it's over."

"You've done this before?" I asked, troubled by the thought.

"Done what? Had this kind of affair? No."

His eyes clouded with guilt, and we both went uncomfortably quiet. But that didn't stop him from driving me deeper into the bed.

The sex got faster and rougher, but I didn't care. I needed the release, too. I clawed his back, leaving scratch marks. My way of branding him, I thought, of making him mine.

The physical pain hadn't subsided, not completely. I was still tender, with his big, thick cock making ramrod motions inside me.

"You're too damned irresistible," he complained. "Too damned beguiling."

So was he, I thought, taking a chance and wrapping my legs

MASQUERADE

around him. In return, he pinned my hands above my head,
cuffing me with his wrists.

Our gazes met and magnified. Were we punishing each
other? Or punishing ourselves?

Lust was a dangerous plight. But love would be far worse.
I tried to tug my hands free, but he wouldn't release me. Fearful of my destiny, I fought harder. He only tightened his grip,
proving that he was stronger.

Bound in body, I thought. Bound in heart.

He slammed his mouth down on mine and kissed me. Our
tongues lashed, and I grew frenzied beneath his demand,
thrashing and quavering.

A climax built in my loins, making me hot and creamy.
For him. For myself. For the affair we weren't supposed to be
having.

Curtis was on the verge of orgasm, too. I felt it in his kiss,
in the shiver of his big, muscular body.

He finally let go of my wrists, and I moaned deep in my
throat, trapped within my release.

A moment later, he pulled out and spilled onto my stomach,
as he'd claimed he would, making me warm and sticky.

We were both breathing heavily, but the roughness was
gone, replaced by a puzzling afterglow. He stroked my cheek,
and I nuzzled the side of his hand.

Naked and still partially erect, he climbed out of bed and

walked to the bathroom to get the materials with which to cleanse me.

While he was gone, I stared dreamily at the ceiling. The pattern was hazy, but pretty, the candle I'd brought adding sparks of light.

He returned, and I fixed my gaze on him. He brought with him a small basin of water and several soft cloths, and he gave me a gentle sponge bath. He even dabbed between my thighs, wiping away the residue of maiden's blood.

When he finished, he balled up the cloths, along with his nightshirt, and I assumed he was going to build a fire later that morning to burn them.

I wanted to stay and cuddle in his arms, but I couldn't. He handed me my dressing gown, and I covered up, preparing to slip back to my suite. I didn't ask if he'd meant what he'd said earlier about doing this again.

Guilty as we were, I knew that we would make love as many dangerous times as we could.

~

Amber knew she was in a dangerous situation. Luke had given her an excruciating orgasm. She'd come desperately against his mouth while he'd been on his knees licking cake from her clit, and Jay had watched the entire scenario.

Now that it was over, Jay had an indiscernible expression

on his masked face, and Luke was standing off to the side, gazing at her through the eyeholes of his equally mysterious mask. As for Amber, her heart was racing. All she wanted was for Luke to fuck her, but that wasn't going to happen. If he put anything inside her, it would be a phallus-shaped object and not the real thing. They'd all agreed on a tongues-and-toys-only night.

"Ready for more?" Jay asked.

She turned in his direction, contemplating his question. Yes, no, maybe? She was back to wishing that she couldn't tell her grooms apart, but it was too late for that. They were who they were.

She responded, "I'm always ready."

Jay persisted. "Are you sure about that? You came pretty hard."

"Girls don't need to recover."

He walked toward her, stopping when he was close enough to whisper, "You always need to recover from Luke."

Amber brought a gentle hand to his jaw, tracing the angles of his Luke-look-alike face. "You're better for me than he is."

"I'm easier for you. Less complicated. That doesn't necessarily mean better."

She glanced over at Luke. She still wanted him inside her. But she needed Jay, too, so she leaned forward and kissed him.

Luke didn't stand idly by. He came up behind Amber and undid the fitting laces on the back of her corset, loosening the ladylike garment.

Although she kept kissing Jay, she was completely aware of her other groom. Finally she and Jay separated, and he turned her around to let Luke open the front of the corset, where hooks and eyes had been keeping it closed.

Upon its removal, Luke lowered his head and sucked on one of her nipples, making her feel like an old-fashioned miss who was about to swoon. She leaned back against Jay for support.

"Told you," he whispered. "He does it to you every time."

She wanted to prove Jay wrong, to insist that she was fine, but Luke was making her downright weak.

Just then, he lifted his head and looked into her eyes, causing her knees to wobble even more.

This time Jay didn't say anything about her reaction to his roommate. Friend that he was, Jay continued to hold her, to give her the support she needed. Without him, she feared she would've faltered.

Luke proceeded to strip her where she stood, discarding her shoes, stockings and barely-there panties. He kept her jewelry in place. She suspected that he liked the bridal statement her pearls and sapphires made.

"Let's take her to bed," he said to Jay.

Yes, let's, Amber thought. She needed to lie down, to be fondled, caressed, ravished.

Whoosh.

Into the master suite they went, where the toys were still strewn upon the quilt.

Luke piled them up and put them on the nightstand. A flesh-colored dildo with anatomical details caught her immediate attention. Had it been one of the objects he'd chosen? Would he use it on her?

Jay turned down the bed, and she climbed under the covers. He got naked and joined her, leaving Luke standing beside the nightstand, still fully clothed.

The Toy Man, she thought.

"Where are the handcuffs?" he asked Jay.

Amber's heart nearly jumped out of her chest. "No restraints." That wasn't part of her fantasy. "I'm not into bondage." It was fine for other women, but not for her.

Luke angled his head. "Don't you trust us?"

She hesitated.

"You told us to pick out whatever we wanted," Luke said.

"I didn't mean handcuffs."

"Don't worry." Jay spoke to Amber, ending the Toy Man's game. "There aren't any."

Her breath rushed out, and she glared at Luke.

"That wasn't funny," she told him.

"I was just teasing you."

Teasing or testing? She'd already let them blindfold her. That was enough control for one night.

"Don't start fighting." This from Jay. "I hate it when you two bicker."

"Who's bickering?" Luke tossed his roommate a glass wand, shaped like a penis and dotted with pink hearts from the base to the tip.

Jay caught it, and Luke said softly to Amber, "I want to watch you kiss it."

She couldn't help it. The hearts fascinated her, and so did Luke. When Jay held it to her lips, she kissed the tip.

Luke said, "More," and she licked the glass, tracing the imprint of the hearts with her tongue.

She liked that he was watching, that he'd provided her with an oddly romantic toy. She licked the entire length, dampening every inch.

When she was done, Jay slid it between her lips and moved it in and out, encouraging her to give it a blowjob. The cool, clear Valentine shape caressed the inside of her mouth.

She glanced over at Luke. Was his cock rubbing against his fly? Was it big and stiff in his pants?

She couldn't deny her excitement. It was wildly arousing to be naked with one groom while the other remained in his wedding gear. Trust Luke to make the scenario work. He might not like being part of a threesome, but he knew how to make Amber feel like a ménage bride.

He probably knew how to make a woman feel like a traditional bride, too. But she wasn't supposed to be thinking along those lines. Tonight she was married to two men.

Luke reached for a bullet vibrator, a tiny device designed for clitoral stimulation.

Jay took the glass wand out of her mouth and helped prepare her for the bullet. He sat upright and held Amber against him, her back to his front.

"Open up," he said. "And show Luke what he wants to see."

She obeyed, spreading herself and exposing her clit. She was still a little sticky from the cake, but that was part of the thrill, the memory, the do-bad-things-to-her wedding night. The masquerade, she thought, that had come unhinged.

While Jay held her, Luke knelt between her legs and studied the vibrator.

"It's supposed to have multi-speed pulsation," he said.

Just hurry up and use it, she thought.

"He drives you nuts," Jay said in her ear.

"Be quiet," she whispered back. She didn't need Groom A giving Groom B more power than he already had.

Luke was still analyzing the bullet. "I've never done this to anyone before. I wonder if it'll feel as good as they say it does." He shifted his attention to Amber. "Do you think it will?"

"Yes," she managed in a slightly cracked voice.

"Do you use stuff like this on yourself?"

"Sometimes."

"I wonder what the record is."

"For what?"

"How many times a woman can come in one night."

Amber had no idea, but she was willing to find out. When he turned it on and placed it against her, she bucked on contact.

At first the vibration was excruciatingly slow, but little by little, he increased the speed. She lifted her hips, struggling to get closer to the device in his hand.

She almost squeezed her eyes shut, but she didn't want to lose sight of her own seduction.

Battery-operated magic.

Already she was on the edge of a mind-blowing, soul-spinning climax. What woman wouldn't react to a vibrator pulsing between her legs?

She told herself it was the toy and not the operator making her shake and shiver. But as she watched him ply her with pleasure, she couldn't deny that she wanted to come for him.

Jay was a significant part of the equation, too. Just having him there, holding her, made her lust for Luke more bearable.

"I know how badly you want him," Jay whispered, zeroing in on her thoughts.

"Don't go there." She couldn't handle having this conversation again.

"Go where?" Luke interrupted, catching her and Jay in the act. "You've been whispering all night."

Jay came clean. "We've been talking about you. Do you want to know what we've been saying?"

Luke paused, then responded, "No," leaving things as they were. But that didn't keep him from frowning.

Amber hissed like a cat. Her world was exploding at her clit, and the man steering her orgasm was as troubled as she was. Their emotional reaction to each other was palpable.

Still holding the bullet in place, he climbed on top of her, kissing her hard and deep.

"You two are hot," Jay said, loud enough for everyone to hear. He was getting squished by the extra weight, but he obviously didn't care. The rough-and-ready chemistry was turning him on.

Amber came in a blur of heat: Luke's thrusting tongue, Jay's probing hands, the device blasting her into another dimension.

But that wasn't her only stimulation. Somewhere in the height of her climax, she fantasized about fucking Luke.

When it ended, no one said a word. They untangled their bodies, and the all-knowing Jay caught her gaze, awareness humming between them.

CHAPTER THIRTEEN

Jay finally broke eye contact, and Amber waited for what would happen next. She struggled with the awkward lull, but what could she do about it? She wasn't in the frame of mind to know what to say.

Luke was, quite obviously, the one in charge. But just as obviously, Jay didn't mind letting his roommate take control. He waited for the next phase, too.

What seemed like another full minute went by. Too much time, Amber thought. Too much silence.

Still no one spoke. But Luke did react. He removed his tuxedo jacket and tossed it onto a vintage armchair angled in the corner.

While he proceeded to undress, Amber's heart did ridiculously girlish things inside her chest.

Anxious, she drew the sheet against her body. Watching Luke peel off his formal attire shouldn't affect her in this way. But it was almost like seeing him naked for the first time.

Once he was bare, she and Jay made room for him in bed. Still silent, the three of them got physically close, warm and sleek under the covers, with Amber in the middle. The burning candles continued to shimmer, creating soft shadows and warm light.

"Déjà vu," Luke said, his voice almost echoing.

He was referring to the first masquerade. Amber understood what he meant, but, for her, the sameness was different. Last time the masked men were practically strangers. Last time she hadn't recited oddly alluring vows.

Groom A. Groom B. Did that make her Bride C?

Curious, she studied Luke, thinking about the nonexistent handcuffs. "So, are you into restraints?"

"No."

"Then what made you tease me about it?"

"I just wanted your reaction, I guess. To see how you'd feel about being captured."

And now he knew. It had scared her.

He put his hand against her cheek. "I'd never do anything to you that you didn't want me to do."

He was being sweetly romantic. Gentle. The man his sisters had shaped him to be. That scared her, too. She almost shivered.

On the other side of her, Jay shifted onto his elbow. He prodded her into challenging Luke. "Tell him what you *do* want."

Fighting the romance, she adhered to Jay's suggestion and looked straight at Luke. "I want you to fuck me."

He lowered his hand. "Not tonight. We made rules."

Jay interjected, "Rules are meant to be broken."

"He's right," Amber said, siding with Groom A. What would she do without Jay? He was her bad-bride champion.

Luke sat up and reached for the anatomically detailed dildo. "I can use this. Will that suffice?"

God, he was stubborn. And beautiful and sexy. He'd chosen the toy of her dirty dreams. She nodded, getting warm between her legs.

"What position do you want her in?" Jay asked.

"Doggie style," Luke responded.

Amber wasn't about to argue. It was exciting to be part of whatever he had in mind.

"Any preference for where I should be?" Jay wanted to know.

"Anywhere you can find a sexy spot."

"It's all sexy." Jay leaned against the headboard. "But I think I'll stay right here. And watch."

Amber climbed to her hands and knees. She looked at Jay. His legs were open, and his cock was half-hard. As for Luke, she couldn't see him. She could hear him, though, ripping into a condom. Clearly, he was rolling it over the toy.

An anxious moment passed, and suddenly she felt softly, strangely exposed. To keep her anxiety in check, she glanced at Jay. He met her gaze, giving her the comfort she sought.

Then Luke leaned over her, making her nerve endings stir. Had he already lubricated the phallus? Already made it warm and slick?

"Are you ready?" he asked.

"Yes."

He kissed the side of her neck, sucking gently, then roughly, then gently again. Was he giving her a hickey? Lord, it felt good.

He sucked a bit more. "We're working on that record."

To make her come as many times as she could? She moaned and closed her eyes. When she opened them, her gaze landed on Jay. He shifted his legs. He was getting harder.

Luke reached down and rubbed the head of the dildo against her. She got instant chills, even though the toy was wonderfully warm.

He inserted it slowly, and the feeling overwhelmed her. He wasn't leaning over her anymore. But he was still close.

He went deeper, and she imagined that the dildo was him.

To heighten the sensation, she gazed at Jay again. By now, he was fully erect.

Luke slid the toy in farther and started to fuck her with it. All the blood from her head rushed to her hands and knees. She rocked her hips, pushing back against the motion.

The bridal fantasy. The wedding ménage. She was staring at Jay's big, beautiful penis and fantasizing about Luke's.

And damn if Jay didn't know it. He flashed a deliberate smile and reached for the lubricant. Slathering it on, he stroked himself, giving her more to fantasize about.

Luke pumped her harder and deeper, sliding the dildo all the way in, then all the way out.

Jay moved his hand up and down. "Remember when you watched him do this?" he asked Amber. "Remember how hard he was for you?"

She clutched the bedding. He was talking about Luke.

"Don't," said Luke to Jay. He'd caught the reference, too.

"Don't what? Make her think about you? Come on, bro, you know you like it."

Luke cursed beneath his breath. Regardless, he continued pushing Amber toward her next climax.

She came for the third time that night, and when she was convulsing, Jay came, too. As for Luke, he gave Amber a moment to breathe, then reached for another toy.

Playing his part to perfection.

~

The following morning, Amber awoke alone in bed.

She sat up and looked around. Thank goodness Luke's and Jay's suitcases were still there. If they'd packed up and left without her, she would've felt horribly jilted. At least her grooms hadn't pulled an Elvis and left the building.

Her grooms?

She ran a hand through her tousled hair. They weren't her husbands anymore. The wedding was over.

She went into the master bathroom to shower and get ready for the day.

Later, she emerged, fashionably groomed, a short summer dress fluttering above her knees.

When she entered the kitchen, Jay greeted her, looking like himself. Any trace of last night's masquerade was gone. She didn't see Luke, but he had to be somewhere nearby.

"I've been waiting for you," Jay said.

"You have?"

"I didn't want to make breakfast until you graced us with your presence."

She smiled. Trust Jay to arrange a home-cooked meal. "You could've ordered in."

"I did order in. I ordered groceries." He motioned to the counter. "Do you want coffee while you're waiting?"

"Sure. Thanks."

He poured her a cup. "Luke is in the garden. In case you're wondering."

"I wasn't." Liar, she thought.

"Just the same. You should let him know that you're up."

"I suppose I should." She doctored her coffee. Seeing Luke shouldn't be a big deal. But she was nervous about it. The garden wasn't a good place for him to be.

"I'll call you guys when the food's ready."

"Thanks. What are we having, by the way?"

"Eggs, potatoes, bacon, French toast, strawberries, fresh cream, the whole shebang." He made a motion with his hands. "Now go. Shoo. Out of my way."

She didn't react to his prompting. She lingered, curious if their "dirty" wedding had done the trick, if he was less inclined to think about Beverly now.

"Go," he said again.

Still, she didn't move. Instead she held her coffee with both hands, still wondering if last night had made a difference for him.

"*Amber.*"

"Okay. Okay." She walked away, wondering if it had made a difference for herself. Had anything changed? Were those old bridal dreams gone for good?

She opened the sliding door, went outside and stood on the

small patio attached to the garden. Luke was seated on a wrought-iron bench just left of the roses. He glanced up, and they stared at each other. He looked fresh and comfy clean. His shirt was a plain white tee, and his jeans had holes in the knees. He was also sporting western boots. It made her wonder if he'd grown up around horses. She had, but her experiences had been elite and showy. His, she suspected, had been simple and earthy.

She lifted her drink. "Jay gave me some coffee."

He raised a matching cup. "Me, too. I'm on my second round."

"Did he tell you what he's fixing for breakfast?"

Luke nodded. "I guess he figures we all need the sustenance after last night."

Amber's skin went flush. She could feel the heat in her cheeks. *Her.* The naughty socialite. Where was the logic in that? "I have to admit, I am hungry."

His hair blew across his forehead. "So am I."

Because she didn't know what else to do, she sipped her coffee. But the hot drink only made her warmer.

"Is it okay if I join you?" she asked.

"Of course you can."

Yes, of course. Stupid question. She moved forward and sat next to him. He'd used every toy on her, every wild device, and now they were behaving ridiculously proper.

"Pretty garden," he said.

"Yes, it is. But I didn't have anything to do with it. The roses, I mean."

"I didn't think you planted them, Amber."

She was still warmer than she should be. Was this how Lady Ellen felt whenever she was around Curtis? Confused? Scattered? "That's not what I meant."

"I know." He finished his coffee and put his empty cup on the ground. "Don't forget that you owe me a date."

When one of the spaghetti straps of her dress slipped onto her shoulder, she righted it quickly. "I haven't forgotten."

"Just so you're aware, I plan on giving you a red rose."

"You've given me too many flowers as it is."

"This one will be different. Special."

He was making her nervous again. She tried to crack a joke. "Guaranteed to get you laid?"

He didn't laugh. "What's wrong with me wanting you?"

To combat her discomfort, she fussed with her other strap, even though it wasn't falling. "You could've had me by now."

"Not without Jay being there."

She struggled to change the subject, but she couldn't think of anything to say that wouldn't increase her anxiety or make her any less attracted to him. So she went silent, hoping that breakfast would be ready soon.

On the morning after I made love with Curtis, I missed breakfast. I missed lunch and dinner, too. In fact, for several days thereafter, I took all of my meals in my suite, feigning an illness.

I was too nervous to face what I'd done. How could I exchange glances with Curtis and not give myself away? Or behave normally around the duke? Or discuss floral arrangements or embroidery patterns with my mother?

Finally, I decided that I had to reemerge and claim to be well again. If I didn't, a doctor would be called and my lie would be in jeopardy. Besides, by now, I was desperate to see Curtis. Concerned as I was about making eye contact with him in the presence of others, he was forever on my mind.

So, on the third day, at breakfast time, I descended the stairs. The duke and Mama seemed grateful that I was well. I managed my composure, but I'd already summoned the courage to be near Curtis.

Soon I learned that he wouldn't be joining us. Wanting to get an early start on his workday, he'd gone into town to purchase supplies. Disappointment clouded my heart.

As we sat down to eat, the duke discussed his schedule. After breakfast, he would be engaged in banking affairs. That was often the case with my fiancé. He was a diligent businessman.

I spent the rest of the morning and earlier part of the after-

noon with Mama. After teatime, I turned fidgety, but Mama didn't reprimand me. She seemed bored. I caught her sighing more times than not.

"I wonder if Mr. Wells would give us a tour of his workspace." I was attempting to conjure an inconspicuous opportunity to see Curtis.

"There's no harm in asking," she responded. "And he did promise that we would be his first guests."

We left the house, and as we strolled across the grounds, a small breeze fluttered, carrying the scent of the sea. Curtis's workshop was near the edge of the property, where the ocean was but a short distance away.

"I wonder about Mr. Wells," Mama said.

My interest piqued. "Wonder what?"

"If he's a man about town."

My heart banged against my breastbone. "Why would that matter?" Was she suspicious of my feelings for him? Of our affair?

"Lady Milford has her sights on him."

I relaxed. "I heard that, too. But she hasn't been around."

"Oh, yes, she has. She dined with us last night."

While I'd been feigning an illness, Lady Milford had been putting her claws into Curtis? "On whose invitation?"

"Her own. She just happened to stop by. The tart."

I made an appropriately shocked sound. "Mama."

"Well, that's what she is."

We both laughed. But for me, the effort was painful. Would Mama think I was a tart, too? And what about Curtis? Was he a man about town? I'd asked him to be faithful to me. But would he be?

"Why did you marry Papa?" I asked suddenly.

Mama stopped walking and gazed uncomfortably at me. I didn't expect her to respond. But she said, "Because I thought he loved me."

Sad inside, I queried her again. "How does a woman know if a man truly loves her?"

"I'm not sure. If I was, I wouldn't have misjudged your father's feelings for me." She reached out to touch my hand. "Are you worried about the duke? About the arrangement of your union?" Assuming the worst, she tried to comfort me. "He appears to care for you, and he seems the sort to fall in love. He doted on his first wife."

"Yes, he claims to have loved her." But it wasn't the duke who was on my mind.

"Then maybe you'll have your turn, too."

"Maybe." But only if Curtis fell in love with me. Already I feared that I was falling in love with him.

Mama didn't comment, but it was just as well, especially since we weren't even discussing the same man.

I resumed walking, and she fell into step with me. We passed the carriage house and came to Curtis's workshop. Mama moved forward to knock on the door. My heart pounded with each and every rap of her hand.

He answered the summons, then stood there, gazing dumbfounded at us.

"Is this a bad time?" Mama asked. "We were hoping to see your shop."

He blinked. "No. No. It's all right. I just didn't know that Lady Ellen had recovered from her illness."

"I'm fine now," I told him.

In actuality, I was far from fine. I wanted to slide straight into his arms. He looked strong and striking in his rough-hewn shirt and dungarees.

"Come in," he said to both of us.

He gave us the tour we requested, showing us his tools and supplies. He also explained the process of his work. I meant to stay focused on what he was saying, but every so often, his gaze deliberately caught mine.

I could tell that he suspected that my illness had been a ruse to avoid our situation. Did he also suspect that I was aware of Lady Milford's pursuit of him?

"I can't wait until you engrave my daughter's name on the pistols," Mama said.

"That's still a ways off," he responded, glancing once again at me.

Recalling the feeling of being naked with him, I smoothed the front of my dress.

Mama spoke again. "I like the way your shop smells."

He turned, smiled at her. "Metal and gun powder?"

Charmed by him, she laughed. "Yes, that must be it." She wandered over to his bench and studied his carving tools. "How long ago did you learn your trade?"

"I apprenticed when I was a boy. I was twelve when I started, twenty-one when I branched out on my own."

"Are you a marksman, too?"

"Yes, ma'am." He exaggerated his drawl. "Fastest gun in the West."

She laughed once more. "It won't be quite as much fun at the estate after you're gone."

"I'm glad you think so. I like it here, too." He stole another glance in my direction. "I plan on working late today. Well into the night."

Was the latter part meant for me? Was it his secretive way of telling me to meet him in his shop after everyone else retired to their chambers?

Heaven to God, I hoped so. There was nothing more I wanted than to rendezvous with him.

For as long as I was able.

CHAPTER FOURTEEN

On the evening of Amber and Luke's date, Jay was working. It was just as well, she thought. He probably would have left them alone anyway.

She turned to study herself in the mirror. Her sleeveless black gown showcased a sweetheart neck and an elegant slit up the side.

Luke was taking her to a club that featured fine dining and ballroom dancing. At the moment, he was waiting in the living room for her.

One last glance and she let out the breath she was holding. She was a playgirl. A bombshell. A diva. She'd been on countless dates with hot, handsome men. This shouldn't be any different.

She entered the living room. He was sitting on the sofa, but he sprang to his feet, reacting like a long, lean, dark-suited panther.

"Fashionably late," she said of herself.

"And gorgeous," he responded.

Amber's pulse picked up speed. He'd called her gorgeous when he'd first seen her in the wedding dress, too. "Thank you."

He reached into his pocket and handed her a snippet of paper with a clear plastic backing. "It's your flower."

She took a closer look. It was a temporary tattoo of a small, delicate rose.

"Luke." She couldn't stop the smile that skirted past her lips.

"I have one, too. But mine is a little different from yours." He pushed up his jacket sleeve and unbuttoned the cuff on his right sleeve. On the inside of his wrist was a red rose twined around a sword.

It made perfect sense for him, she thought. The knight, the groom, prepared to fight off attackers while he held his lady.

"It looks authentic." She took a second glance. "It's not, is it?" Had he gotten inked for real? That actually seemed like something he would do.

"No. It's temporary."

She was glad that he hadn't made the rose thing between

them permanent. She was having enough trouble with the way he made her feel.

"Let's put yours on." He scanned the length of her. "Where do you think it should go?"

"Here." Instantly she chose a spot to the left of her breast because she thought it would look good with her sweetheart neckline.

But once Luke started to apply the tattoo, she realized how close it was going to be to her heart. Too late to backpedal. The tattoo would be visible soon.

About thirty seconds later, he peeled off the paper backing and rinsed the rose with water.

While it was drying, he said, "It looks beautiful on you."

She thanked him, then asked, "How long will it last?"

"About a week. Unless you decide to remove it before then."

"Are you going to remove yours before the week is up?"

"I'll probably wait it out."

"Then I probably will, too." A decision she hoped she wouldn't regret.

He leaned in to kiss her, making the placement of the rose seem even more intimate.

Afterward, they left the house and drove to their destination. Mostly they were silent in the car.

At the club, they were seated on a glass-enclosed rooftop, making the atmosphere seem magical. The view was spectacular.

The well-dressed clientele came in all ages, shapes and sizes. At the adjacent table was an elderly couple who looked as if they'd been together forever.

Upon surveying the menu, Amber and Luke chose crab cakes as an appetizer and filet mignon as main courses. She went for the house salad, and he opted for a traditional Caesar. Neither ordered wine or cocktails, and she wasn't sure why. Maybe they needed to be in control of their senses tonight?

Before things got quiet again, she started a conversation. "This is an interesting club. I like the retro vibe."

"It seemed like a good place for a date, especially since I want to dance with you. But I haven't waltzed in a while. I'll probably be a little rusty."

"I think you'll do just fine." As far as she was concerned, he seemed to do everything well, especially if it involved romance.

The appetizer arrived, followed by their salads. By the time their steaks were served, Amber was looking into Luke's eyes and wishing that she wasn't. He had a mesmerizing effect on her, yet another facet of his boy-seduces-girl skills.

"Tell me about your childhood," he said.

She poked at the food on her plate. "You want details about my daddy issues?"

"Yes, I do. We agreed to talk about it sometime, remember?"

Yes, she remembered. "It's not that complicated. I just wanted more from my father than I got. And when Daddy went away, I started wanting more from my step-dads, all three of them, and when they went away and Mama quit re-marrying, I was old enough to know better."

Luke backtracked. "More of what, Amber? Love? Attention? Affection?"

She thought for a moment, *really* thought about it. "I wanted to trust them, but they weren't the trustworthy sort."

"Your mom always married the same type of man?"

"I don't think she did it purposefully." Amber cut into her steak, wondering if this was a good time to wield a knife. "I was supposed to be Daddy's little girl, his princess, but it was just talk. Whenever I was home from boarding school, we would plan my wedding."

"Ah, so that's how it got started."

She nodded. "We would talk and talk about it. About how someday he would walk me down the aisle. About how special that day would be." She glanced at the dance floor. The band was just setting up to play. "He would even elaborate on the father/daughter dance. But he was always doing that. Making himself out to be the big hero when in actuality he was barely around. Two weeks before my tenth birthday, Mama caught him in bed with her best friend."

"I'm sorry," Luke said sincerely. "For you and your mom."

"My parents split up, and he found even less and less time to be my daddy, until he drifted away for good. So I clung to my stepfathers. 'Will you always be my daddy?' I would ask. 'Of course I will' each of them would reply. But they didn't stick around, either. None of them are part of my life now."

"Leaving no one to walk you down the aisle."

She didn't respond. Mostly because she didn't know what to say.

He asked, "When did you design the dress?"

"When I was sixteen. By then I knew what would look glamorous on me. That I was the sheath type."

He caught her gaze from across the table. "It was the right choice. I've never seen a more stunning bride."

Amber's mind whirred, but Luke had that effect on her. "I was still a virgin when I designed it. Saving myself for my wedding night."

She should have laughed at the irony, but she didn't. Neither did he. They just sat there, looking at each other.

Finally he said, "Not all men are like the men your mom married."

"What are you saying, Luke? That someday I'll find a guy who won't abandon me?"

He nodded.

"Someone like you?" she asked, putting him on the spot.

He didn't flinch. But he didn't quite breathe, either. "Jay probably thinks so."

"Jay's mixed up."

"We all are. I've known that from the beginning."

"It doesn't matter. When I leave, it'll be over." Temporary, she thought, like the tattoos they were both wearing.

"It matters for now," he responded softly.

She didn't say anything back to him, and they finished their meals in romantic silence.

When she reached for her soda and took a sip, she wished that she'd ordered an erotic-named cocktail, like she'd done at the strip club. This date seemed much too innocent. She felt sixteen again.

As the band began to play a lovely rendition of "The Love Theme from Romeo and Juliet," she worried that it was a good/bad omen. The classic Franco Zeffirelli movie, from which the song originated, as well as the modern Baz Luhrmann version, counted as two of her all-time favorite films.

She glanced at the older couple at the adjacent table. They were getting out of their seats and heading for the dance floor. She noticed that they wore matching wedding bands. She was probably right about them being together forever.

Luke glanced their way, too. Then he turned back to Amber. "Should we join them?"

Her heart fluttered in her chest. She told her sixteen-year-old self it was the music. "Okay."

Luke stood up, came around to her side and pulled back her chair.

She couldn't help her reaction. She looked up at him and smiled. "Chivalry is alive and well."

He smiled, too, and flicked his wrist. "It must be the sword."

She got to her feet. The song for her and the sword for him. They were quite a pair.

What happened next didn't surprise her. He took her in his arms, and they danced beautifully together.

As they swept past the older couple, Amber wondered about them. Did they like living in the same house, sleeping in the same bed, watching the same television shows and socializing with the same friends?

Shifting her thoughts, she focused on the man leading her through what seemed like an effortless waltz.

But in reality, nothing was effortless, at least nothing that involved a relationship.

Luke was wrong. She wouldn't find a man who wouldn't abandon her because she wasn't interested in finding one. Being sensuously single made more sense.

Clothes-optional resorts. Jet-setting parties. Wild three-somes. No way could an old married couple top that.

Song after song, she and Luke danced, right along with the gray-haired pair. After more people drifted onto the floor, Luke asked Amber if she wanted to return to the table and order dessert.

She almost declined, but this wasn't a dance-off. If the older couple wanted to stay in each other's aging arms, it was their prerogative.

Once they were seated, Amber and Luke scanned the dessert menu.

He said, "I can't decide between the Black Forest torte and the strawberry charlotte."

"I was thinking the same thing."

"Then we'll get one of each and share them." He looked up from the menu. "Okay?"

"Sure." She met his gaze, remembering what he'd done to her with the wedding cake. "Coffee, too?"

"Decaf. Or else we'll never sleep tonight."

"Am I staying in your room?"

"Absolutely. All I want is you with me."

She went coy. "That's not all you want."

"You're right. I'll take as much as I can get."

"And with me, you'll get plenty." Plenty of foreplay, plenty of sex. She glanced at the dance floor, where the older couple still swayed.

But never plenty of love.

~

As I dressed for the night, wrapping a shawl around my shoulders, I tried to formulate a plan—an explanation for going on an outing at this hour, should someone awaken and see me.

Maybe I could say that I required the cool night air to cleanse my lungs after my illness. A long, solitary walk on the estate grounds, with a lantern in tow so I didn't stumble in the dark.

Yes, I thought. It was as good excuse as any.

As I crept down the stairs, I was overly aware of the wood creaking beneath me. Had the stairwell ever been this noisy before?

I reached the bottom and stood very still, debating which to way to go. I looked this way and that. With a sharp yet cluttered mind, I walked toward the breakfast room, where glass doors led to the garden. It seemed safer, less conspicuous than the front entrance or kitchen door, which was much too close to the maids' quarters.

Once I was in the garden, I breathed in the heady scent of nocturnal blooms. The path to Curtis's workshop was in the other direction, so I cut across the grass and held my lantern up a little higher to light the way.

A part of me wanted to run, but making a mad dash for the man of my dreams wasn't prudent. I was supposed to be cleansing my lungs with the night air.

The walk seemed to take forever, but my sense of time was skewed. This wasn't my usual hour to be out and about. I glanced back and noticed that the moon floated along in the same direction, as if following my lead.

My hair blew about my shoulders because I'd worn it long and loose. I wanted to feel free, but I wasn't. My heart was trapped like a caged animal.

My fear of loving Curtis.

When his shop came into view, I released a shaky breath. A light shined from inside. He was indeed there, waiting for me, I hoped. If I'd misinterpreted what I'd assumed had been an invitation, I would feel the fool.

As my mother had done earlier that day, I knocked on the door, only I did it ever so softly.

But not too softly for him not to hear.

He opened the door, and I went inside. I set the lantern on his workbench and removed my wrap. Wordless we gazed at each other.

Then I said, "I wasn't ill," admitting what he most likely already knew. "I needed time to compose myself. I was afraid I would give us away."

"But you didn't. You haven't."

As I stood within touching distance of him, I considered what had happened in my absence. "I heard that Lady Milford came to see you."

"I'm not interested in her." He paused. *"You're all I've been thinking about. Day and night. Only you."*

The intensity with which he looked at me was overwhelming. Was I in the midst of my own dream?

I reached for him, and he took me in his arms. Our mouths came together in a heated exchange. He tasted like everything I wanted, everything I needed. I couldn't imagine existing without him.

When the kiss ended, I said, "What am I going to do when you're gone?"

His body was still close to me. "Don't talk about that. Not now. Let's just be together when we can, as often as we can."

Could I keep slipping away to meet him? Could I keep perpetuating our sin?

He read the expression in my eyes. "I wish I could give you more than this."

I feigned the innocence he'd already taken from me. "More than what?"

Smiling at my attempt at humor, he slid his hands down and cupped my bottom, tugging my pelvis against his.

We kissed once again, and this time, he lifted me up and sat me on the edge of his workbench, making me part of his environment.

"Raise your skirt," he said.

I obeyed him, and he removed my drawers, leaving me

bare beneath my garment. He moved closer and put his hand between my legs, using his fingers in a wicked way.

In and out he went, penetrating me with one, then two digits. I gazed him at him the entire time. He never failed to make me wanton.

In the middle of his foray, he removed his fingers and brought them to my lips.

"Taste yourself," he told me.

I should have been embarrassed, but I wasn't. Being sinful with him was what I'd been born to do. I licked and sucked, savoring the tangy flavor. I behaved like a cat cleaning another cat's milky paws.

Through fluttering lashes, I watched his reaction. He was more aroused than ever. He opened the front of his dungarees and freed his erection.

I shifted closer to the edge of his workbench, but he didn't enter me. He fumbled around in his pocket and produced a condom. I'd never seen one up close, but I understood its function.

"These are difficult to get in America now," he said. "But they're readily available here. I bought enough to last a while."

"When did you get them?"

"When I went into town. But don't fret. No one knows who my partner is."

"*They'll probably think you're having relations with Lady Milford.*"

"*They can think whatever they want so long as you and I are together.*" *He fitted himself with the condom and reached down to make me wet again.*

I sighed from his stimulation. He was right. All that mattered was the two of us.

As he slid his sheathed length inside me, I wrapped my legs around him, my skirt bunching between us. At that wildly intimate moment, I shed my fear and accepted the notion of loving him.

Sensing that he was falling in love with me, too.

CHAPTER FIFTEEN

After dessert, Luke took Amber to the beach. It wasn't the most ideal place for formalwear, but the sand and the surf and the moonlight had come calling, and he was spontaneous enough to answer it.

Immersed in the moment, he asked, "Do you want to go for a walk?"

"That sounds nice." She removed her heels and placed them on the dashboard, where they made a sleek, feminine statement.

Following her lead, he discarded his shoes and socks. He also rolled up his pant legs.

Once they were standing outside the car, he offered her his jacket.

"You're being chivalrous again," she said.

"It's the least I can do, considering my lady's feet are bare."

She accepted his jacket, and he helped her into it.

Afterward, she said, "Lady Amber and Sir Luke. Is that who we are tonight?"

"If that's who you want us to be."

"I don't know what I want. But you've been making me feel like I did when I was a teenager."

Dreamy, he thought. Idyllic. The girl saving herself for her wedding night.

He took her hand, and they strolled along the sand. The ocean rolled upon the shore in foamy waves. By morning, it would be laden with surfers.

"Do you think Curtis and Lady Ellen ever did this?" she asked.

"Walked on the beach? I'd like to think they did. They certainly will in my story."

She stopped and turned toward him. "What's it like to create characters in your mind?"

He smoothed a strand of her blowing hair. "I'm not creating them. They were real."

"A woman who'd been exiled, and a man who'd been shot and killed. That's a lot of tragedy in the name of lust."

He corrected her. "It was in the name of love."

"So the story goes. But who really knows for sure?"

"I'll bet your family believes it."

"Mama does, but I think that was her downfall. She was forever searching for her own Curtis."

"The husband mishaps?"

Amber nodded. "I guess she hadn't stopped to consider Curtis's failed marriage or the way he abandoned his child."

"I understand how personal that feels to you, but I think if he'd had a chance to live, he would have righted his wrong. He would've reunited with his daughter and proved himself a good father."

"You're giving him more credit than he deserves."

"He's related to you on your mother's side."

"The good side?"

"Exactly."

While she appeared to contemplate his reasoning, he took the liberty of kissing her, of putting his hands inside her jacket—his jacket—and skimming her curves.

She moaned and moved closer, intensifying the feeling. He knew better than to think that this was anything but lust. Yet, as he and Amber locked lips on the beach, with the sea crashing in their ears, he wondered if Jay was right.

Was Luke half in love with her?

Christ, he thought, with a bolt of panic. No man in his

right mind would fall in love with Amber Pontiero. She was rich and spoiled and emotionally damaged. Commitment to her was two masked men and a phony wedding night.

He pulled back to clear his head.

"What's wrong?" she asked.

"Nothing." Did she have to sound so soft? So angelic? Like the innocent girl she'd once been? "I just needed to catch my breath."

"You look scared."

He frowned. "Of what?"

"I don't know. Of our date, maybe. Of this romantic path you've been leading me down."

Clever observation, he thought.

"It's okay if you don't want to do this, Luke. We can go home and climb into bed with Jay."

"Screw that." Masculine envy jabbed him straight in the gut. "We're seeing this through. Besides, I'm the first one you married."

"With a cock ring," she reminded him.

He didn't care if had been with a cigar band. He wasn't sharing her, not this time. He needed one night that was his, one fantasy that didn't involve another man. "You're making love with me, and you're sleeping in my arms."

"Yes, sir." She said it sarcastically.

"That's Sir Luke to you."

She rolled her eyes, and in the next instant they both laughed. Silly as it was, at least it broke the tension.

"So, are we good now?" he asked.

She nodded. "I want you inside me. I always have."

That was all it took for him to feel knightly again. He scooped her up and carried her to the car, anxious to get her home and straight into his bed.

~

"Walk with me," Curtis said.

We'd just made love in his shop, and now neither of us was able to say good-bye for the night. "Where shall we go?"

He gestured in the direction of the sea. "Out there, my lady."

Where we would meld into the shadows, I thought. Entranced, I smoothed the front of my skirt and reached for my wrap. "That's a lovely idea."

He smiled and leaned over to give me a sweet kiss. "Our moonlight awaits."

Indeed it did. We left his shop and headed toward the ocean, the night bathed in a soft glow.

Once we arrived at the shore, we walked along the sand, our footsteps silent. The water made frothing waves, and a salty breeze nipped the air.

"It's beautiful here," he said.

"It is." I appreciated my homeland, but it wouldn't be the same once he was gone. If only we could stay together.

"What's your favorite sea creature?" he asked.

"Real or imaginary?"

"Real."

I thought for a moment, then responded, "The seahorse. I read that they mate for life, and that every morning they come together and dance, changing colors and twirling around with their tails entwined."

"What happens after they dance?"

"They separate for the rest of the day." I enlightened him with more of my scientific knowledge. "And how amazing is this? The male seahorse can have babies."

He laughed at my wonder. "That sounds terrible to me."

I laughed, too. "I suppose it would to a man." I quickly frowned. "The duke is marrying me to give him an heir."

"That's a common reason for a nobleman to take a bride."

"Yes, but it should be for love."

When Curtis fell silent, I sensed his troubled mind.

Finally he said, "My wife was with child when we wed."

"You conceived your daughter out of wedlock?"

"Yes. But I didn't love her mother. Not in the way I should have."

I gripped the edges of my shawl, for it was threatening to whip in the wind. "At least you tried to do right by her."

"But I failed. As a husband. As a father." His voice went rough, deep with emotion. "My daughter deserves better than me."

I got emotional, too. "That's poppycock. You're a good man, Curtis, and your daughter deserves to have you in her life."

"Do you really believe that?"

"Of course, I do."

"On what account?"

"On the account of being your lover." I would bear a hundred of his babies if he would let me. "And on the account of my father."

"Your father is a louse."

"Precisely." I stood toe to toe with him. "If Papa was half the man you are, I would be proud to call him my own."

"You're a woman to reckon with, Lady Ellen."

"Does that mean you'll visit Sophie when you return to the States?"

He didn't respond, but I could tell that he was touched by our conversation, by the importance of it.

In the silence that followed, we both turned toward the ocean. He reached for my hand, and with each moment that passed, I fell deeper in love with him.

"My favorite sea creatures are starfish," he said.

I considered his choice. "I like them, too. They look rather magical. I wonder if they can be wished upon, like the stars in the heavens."

"I don't see why not. A wish is a wish."

Yes, but did they ever come true? So far, none of mine had. Not unless I included this night as one of them.

"What about mythical sea creatures?" I asked. "Which of those do you fancy?"

"A bare-breasted siren would be nice."

"Mr. Wells." I scolded him, but I smiled, too. "That's wicked."

"Okay, then a sea serpent, the kind that demands virgins as a sacrifice."

I swatted his arm, teasing him, enjoying him. "You're a rogue."

"So I am. But thanks to me, at least you won't get eaten by the serpent."

I shouldn't have laughed, but I did. "In your next life, you're coming back as a seahorse." I poked the flatness of his male stomach. "With little offspring in your pouch."

"Now who's being wicked?" He swept me into a mock-kissing position, bending me backwards like a bow.

I looked up at him, and suddenly we stopped jesting. He righted my posture, and I put my head on his shoulder, burying my cheek against him.

He stroked a hand down my hair, comforting me for the way we felt about each other.

And for the words we didn't have the courage to say.

~

As soon as Amber was alone in Luke's room with him, she went into panic mode, similar to the way he'd reacted at the beach.

But she had a right to her turn.

Before they undressed, before they kissed, before he turned her into a pile of mush, she said, "I'm going to do this with Jay, too."

He frowned. "Do what?"

"Be alone with him."

"Are you trying to kill the moment?"

Yes? Maybe? Sort of? "I just wanted to remind you that I agreed to be with him, too. Remember, we all talked about it on the first day I arrived?"

He looked straight at her, yet his eyes seemed hooded. But there had always been a sense of mystery about Luke. Prince Charming with an edge. She supposed Curtis bore the same confusing quality.

"This isn't the time to discuss you and Jay," he said.

"Okay, but I just wanted to clear the air."

"Fine." His jaw tensed. "Consider it cleared."

"You won't fight me on it later?"

Although he hesitated, he said, "No. I won't."

She couldn't think of anything else to say, so she kept

quiet. Her heart was pounding faster than it should be, and she hated the feeling.

"Do you still want me inside you?" he asked.

She nodded, wishing that she didn't.

"Then take off your dress."

She held her breath and reached back to undo her zipper, uncomfortable about the way she'd confided in him earlier. "My first time wasn't as innocent as you probably think it was." Determined to retain her playgirl image she added, "I seduced the guy I was with, and it was easy for me to reel him in. I'd always gotten by on how I looked. Sex was just a new facet of it."

"Why are you telling me this?"

"Because it seems like something you might want to know. You and your psychobabble stuff."

Luke didn't comment on her answer. Instead, he asked, "What's taking you so long to get out of your dress?"

Amber made a face. "The zipper's stuck."

He almost smiled, and she realized how contrary she must seem: the femme fatale fumbling with her designer gown.

"Turn around," he told her.

She presented him with her back, and he came forward and opened the garment. *Ziiiip.* Just like that, it behaved for him.

As the dress slid to the floor, he unhooked her strapless bra and let it fall, too.

"You do your panties," he said, still standing behind her.

Shedding her underwear should've been second nature, but self-consciousness had crept in. Regardless, she peeled them off and turned to face him, refusing to let her sudden insecurity show.

He roamed the length of her, not with his hands, but with his pitch-dark gaze. "Who was he, Amber? And how old were you?"

She assumed he was referring to her first time. "He was a shipping heir. I was nineteen, and he was twenty."

"Did it happen again?"

"With him? No."

"It was a one-night stand?"

"That's how I wanted it." No rituals. No pomp and circumstance. No repeat performance.

This time, he reached out to caress her, to stroke her bared flesh. "I've never devirginized anyone."

She swayed from his touch. He would be good at it. Too good, she thought. Too caring. She wouldn't have chosen him as her first.

"What was it like for you?" she asked.

"My first time?" He circled her nipples, rubbing them with his thumbs. "Men aren't supposed to kiss and tell."

"Come on, Luke. Just tell me something about who you were with, something to satisfy my curiosity."

"She was older than I was."

"How much older?"

"Old enough to show me what women like."

"Then I guess I should thank her."

He backed her against the footboard. "You can send her a note when we're done."

"Wouldn't she be surprised?" In spite of their banter, her pulse was doing triple time. He was removing his clothes, and he had an erection from here to Texas.

They climbed into bed, and she shivered from being so dangerously close to him.

No toys, she thought. No tricks. Just two people, flesh to flesh. She struggled not to panic.

As he nuzzled his way down her body, she relaxed. He had the good sense to use his skills and put his face between her legs, making her forget how romantically terrified she was.

She scooted closer, and he looked up at her, making a naughty connection. She watched him tongue her clit—small swirls, long dragging licks. His technique was relentless.

Breathy sounds escaped her throat.

He raised the stakes, putting his fingers inside her, thrusting with sweet intensity. She got hot and wet and sticky. The combination from her juices and his saliva made her crazy. Him, too. She could see the passion in his eyes.

She thrust her hips, and he teased them both, removing his fingers and drawing circles on her stomach with the wetness.

But even so, his mouth never left her clit. Enthralled, she tunneled her hands through his hair, tugging at the thickness. He had beautiful hair, but she supposed it was the Choctaw in him.

He licked and licked, and the warmth of his tongue was more than she could bear. She came in rippling waves, relishing the delicious sensation. One last pant, one last tug of his hair, and she wondered if she really should send the woman who'd taught him a thank-you note.

In the hazy aftermath, he kissed her, much too tenderly, leaving her breathless.

As they lay limb to limb, he searched her gaze. "Do you need a minute?"

She nodded, and the notion that she required recovery time wasn't in her best interest. She was actually nervous about him putting his cock inside her.

"Just tell me when you're ready."

"Now," she answered quickly. If she kept waiting, kept recovering, the anticipation would worsen.

He trailed a finger down the center of her body. "What position do you want to do first?"

"I'm not sure." She felt as if she was about to lose her cherry all over again, only this time she was in peril of getting emotionally attached. "What do you want to try?"

"Everything. But I want you on top the most."

So she could impale herself, inch by excruciating inch?

He leaned over and removed protection from the nightstand drawer. He handed it to her, giving her the honor.

She cursed her fumbling fingers. On an average day, she could apply a condom with her eyes closed or her hands tied behind her back. But tonight she could barely get the dang thing out of the packet.

"Don't be scared," he said.

She turned the tables on him. "You freaked out at the beach."

"I know. But it's just one night. One fantasy. There's no reason for either of us to overreact." He took the condom and put it on. "Now climb on board and let me watch."

She straddled him, and he circled her waist, anxious for it to happen.

Amber was anxious, too. She took him from tip to shaft, slowly, beautifully. Fear had never felt this amazing. That, in itself, was scary, but she refused to let it spoil the moment.

He watched her, and she watched him. When he arched his body, she admired his long, lean muscles.

As she rode him, his cock flared inside her. She moved in a languid rhythm, fondling his balls as she came down on him.

He rose up to kiss her, and she let him sweep her into the dreaminess he'd created.

They weren't fucking, she thought. They were making love, just as he'd planned.

But by morning, it would be over and they could both breathe easily again.

With no more romantic feelings between them.

CHAPTER SIXTEEN

As daylight flirted with the blinds and illuminated Luke's room, he waited for Amber to awaken. Only he wasn't exactly sure why he was waiting or what he expected to happen.

Their date was over.

Still, he couldn't seem to get up and start his day without making a morning-after connection with her. Maybe he wanted an exchange of words, a verification that it really was over.

They'd slept soundly, their naked bodies pressed close. Even now, one of her legs was touching his.

He waited and waited, and by the time she stirred, he was leaning against the headboard, his lower half covered with a sheet. He wanted to kiss her, but he didn't.

She didn't offer him a kiss, either. She merely sat up and

settled next to him, naked as the day she was born. He glanced at her beautiful body, then lifted his gaze.

After a jigger of heart-deafening silence, she said, "Hi."

He managed a "Hi" in return.

She rubbed her eyes, and the sleepy gesture made her seem assailable. But he wasn't out to conquer her. Was he?

"I wonder if Jay's home," she said.

Luke didn't try to temper the rivalry. It hit him too fast. "Why does it matter if he's here?"

"I'm craving one of his breakfasts."

Was that all she was craving from Jay? Luke frowned at her, and she lifted the blanket, cloaking her nakedness. Had she covered up purposefully? His brain was too scrambled to know the difference between coy and calculating.

He went on the attack. "It isn't Jay's job to cook for you."

She went on the defense. "I've never heard him complain about it. In fact, when I first came here, he offered to be my chef."

"Not every day."

She huffed out a breath. "What's wrong with you?"

"I'm just making a point." And picking a fight, he supposed. But he couldn't seem to help it.

"I think you're jealous of Jay."

"Because he can cook? The way to a woman's heart isn't through her stomach."

"Says who?"

"Says me." Annoyed by her uncharacteristic modesty, he tore the blanket away from her. "And quit covering up."

"Fine. Then you, too." She pulled the sheet away from his hips.

They looked at each other, and he cursed beneath his breath. Anger was turning to lust, and he was getting hard. She glanced down, and his cock all but jumped.

"Don't even think about it," she said.

"Try and stop me." He lunged forward and captured her mouth.

She dug her nails into his shoulders, but she didn't push him away. She kissed him back, her tongue sparring with his. It was hot and brutal, and he craved as much as he could get.

They rolled over the bed, roughly putting their hands on each other. Finally they quit tussling. He was fully erect and desperate to fuck.

He grabbed a rubber and thrust it at her. "Can you handle it this time?"

"I can handle anything you can dish out." She opened the packet and put the condom in her mouth, holding a portion of it with her teeth.

Next she lowered her head and rolled the condom over the tip of his penis with her tongue. Christ, he thought. No one had ever done that to him before.

She kept going, following the shape of him with her mouth.

She went all the way to the end of his shaft, covering him completely and expertly.

When she lifted her head, she challenged him with an arrogant gaze. He almost pushed her down again. But it wasn't a blowjob he was after.

"I deserve a commendation for that," she said.

"What? Like a Girl Scout badge? I don't think that's part of the curriculum."

"Really? Oh, I thought it was."

Sleek and sexy, she climbed on top of him. He decided that he wanted her sprawled out beneath him, so he switched positions, going missionary. But he did it sinfully, nudging her legs apart with his knees.

Amber reached back and grabbed a hold of the headboard. Was she preparing for a bumpy entrance? He hoped so, because he couldn't slow down if he tried.

Quick and rough, he thrust into her, pounding her so hard, he was probably making her teeth rattle.

She liked it as much as he did. She let go of the wood and snaked herself around him like a viper.

It was the most intense sex he'd ever had. As he moved in and out, they exchanged dirty words and kissed sloppily.

She clutched his ass, and he pounded into her, both of their bodies taking a venomous beating. She even hissed in his ear when she came.

His world exploded at his cock, and he came, too, lost in the merciless act. At the very end, he kissed her one last time, nearly swallowing her mouth whole.

When he collapsed in her arms, they panted in unison.

Luke got up to dispose of the condom. Afterward, he returned to bed, preparing to hold her. Then something inside him snapped worse than it already had, and he realized that he was in trouble.

Deep, deep shit.

As she stretched her long, lethal body, he braced himself on his elbows and stared down at her.

The panic from the beach came back. Tenfold.

He wanted to deny it, to say it wasn't so. But he couldn't. He felt it in his bones, in his twisted heart, in his screwed-up head.

He loved her. He actually loved her. Of all people, of all women, why did it have to be her?

"Quit looking at me like that," she said.

He squinted, trying to make her gorgeous image disappear. "Like what?"

"Like you're pissed off again."

He was—at himself, at her, at Jay. "You're not going to do it. I won't let you."

"Do what?"

"Have a one-on-one with Jay." Luke knew better than to

try to make things work with Amber, but he didn't want his roommate to have her, either. Just the thought of them being alone together tore at his gut.

Naturally, she refused to listen. "I'll do whatever I please."

He grabbed her wrists and cuffed them with his hands. "Not if I can help it."

"Well, you can't." She struggled against him. "Last night you said that you wouldn't fight me about this."

"So I changed my mind."

"Who I sleep with isn't up to you."

She kept trying to break free, but he refused to let go. Finally, he decided it was pointless and released her.

Not to be outdone, she shoved him away and stormed out of bed to search for her clothes. Finding them on the floor, she donned her bra and panties and held her rumpled dress against her.

He got up, as well, and put on his underwear. Arguing in the buff wasn't his idea of fun, either. None of this was. All he wanted was his heart back.

She turned away and flung open the door, and there stood Jay on the other side. He was in his Skivvies, too.

"What's going on?" the other man asked. "I could hear you two snapping at each other all the way down the hall."

Amber responded, "Luke's pissed off because he doesn't want me to be alone with you."

Jay had a simple solution. "Then don't be with me."

Amber argued. "But you said that you wanted time alone."

"I did when you first got here. But it doesn't matter anymore. Especially if it's going to cause a fight."

She rounded on Jay. "You're taking Luke's side? I should have known. You really are like brothers." She divided her gaze between them. "You can both go to hell."

Like the drama queen she was, she pushed past them and headed for their room.

"She's going to pack to go home," Jay said.

"I know."

"You need to stop her."

"No I don't."

"Why? Because you're scared? Because you finally figured out that you love her? Jesus, man, get a grip."

Luke wanted to punch his roommate, sock him right in the face. But he said, "If you tell her, I'll kill you."

"Gee, thanks for being grateful."

"For what? Not being alone with her? I appreciate what you did. But it doesn't change the fact that she needs more than one man."

"I think she's as scared as you are."

Again, her fear didn't change the facts. "Quit being a love guru and let it go."

"I'm not making any promises, bro. I'll tell her if I feel like it."

"Fuck you, then. Or go fuck her." At this point, Luke told himself that he didn't give a damn, even if he still did.

Jay wouldn't back off. "I only wanted to be with her to help forget about Beverly."

"That's the same reason you wanted to do the wedding night."

"Yeah, and it didn't work. I might be locked in the past, but you're screwing up your future."

Right, Luke thought. His loss. His future. His choice.

～

I didn't have a choice. I couldn't stop what was happening.

Lady Milford was doing her flirtatious best to steal Curtis away from me, and she wasn't even aware that he was mine.

Earlier today, the duke hosted a picnic on the lawn with a gathering of friends, including Lady Milford.

The picnic itself had been a disaster. Much to the duke's dismay, the weather had turned unpredictable, and a burst of rain splattered us all.

He'd quickly moved the party indoors, where it was still in progress. Unfortunately, most of the ladies had suffered a loss of vanity, with damaged coiffures and water-speckled dresses.

Lady Milford didn't seem to care. She'd laughed playfully

as the rain fell, latching onto Curtis as everyone made a mad dash for the house.

She hadn't left his side since. As for me, I kept my distance, smiling at the duke whenever necessary. But deep inside, I feared my face was about to crack. Every time I caught sight of Lady Milford hanging on to Curtis's arm, I wanted to cry.

On occasion, he would glance my way with an apology in his eyes. He knew better than to scorn the widow publicly, so he tolerated her affection.

But I was still envious, not so much of her, but of what she represented: the freedom to pursue Curtis without repercussions.

If they became lovers—and everyone at the party probably already thought they were—no ill will would come her way.

At the moment she was nibbling on a small fruit-filled cake and listening to Curtis entertain a group of people with one of his American stories. The gunsmith was charming the towel-dried guests, and the tart was eating a tart.

I sat on a settee by myself, sipping tea and watching the man I loved. We still hadn't said the words to each other, but our feelings were clear.

Of course, what did it matter, if we had no future? Within no time, Curtis would be back in Texas, and I would be in the throes of planning my wedding, with the duke finalizing every decision I made. Not that I cared. The ceremony meant nothing to me.

Nor was I the blushing bride the duke had bought and paid for. During the consummation, I would be forced to playact, becoming a virgin once again. I'd even thought of a story to tell. In the dark of night, I would shyly proclaim that I'd lost my maidenhead in a horseback riding incident. I didn't want to lie; I didn't want to pretend that I hadn't had Curtis inside me, but what else could I do? If the duke knew the truth, he would cast me and my parents out on the street. I wasn't worried about myself or Papa, but Mama was too frail to survive poverty. She needed the duke's charity.

Still focused on Curtis, I sighed. In the past week, we'd been sneaking off almost every night to be together, craving the warmth of each other's arms.

As I placed my teacup and saucer on a side table, he took leave from the group gathered around him. He even escaped Lady Milford.

He stared straight at me, then turned and headed down the nearest corridor. The other guests probably assumed he was en route to one of the downstairs water closets, but I knew otherwise. The look he'd given me was an invitation to join him.

But where?

I waited a beat, stood up, smoothed my skirt and attempted to walk in the same direction. But before I arrived at the corridor, Lady Milford caught my attention.

"This is a lovely party," she said to me.

"Thank you, but I feel a fright." I patted my weather-mussed coiffure. "Rain doesn't become me."

"Only a few curls are out of place."

"Is that all? It feels so much worse."

"Truly it isn't."

"Still, I think I should try to repair the damage now that my hair has dried."

"Yes, of course." She administered a long, sweeping glance. "You're the future lady of the manor, and the duke expects only the best."

Was it my imagination or did she suspect that I was being disloyal to my betrothed?

No, I thought. She would never bestow that kind of credit on someone like me. She would never think that I was wild enough to take a lover, least of all the man she'd set her seductive sights on.

"Go," she said, treating me like a child. "Pretty yourself up, and I'll speak with you later. Far be it from me to keep you from your repair."

I wanted to tell her to stuff her face with another tart, but, naturally, I held my tongue. Making a deliberate enemy of Lady Milford wouldn't do.

I thanked her and excused myself. But as I walked away, I got an unsettling feeling that she was watching me.

The thought made me shiver, so I summoned the courage

to check. I gazed over my shoulder and discovered that I was wrong. She wasn't paying me any mind.

I relaxed and continued on my way, desperate to see Curtis.

To touch him, I thought, to kiss him, as many times as I could.

～

Amber wanted Luke to stop her from leaving, yet at the same time, she never wanted to see him again.

Confusion 101.

He messed with her mind, making her long for fantasies that belonged to her youth, ideals she couldn't recoup.

One man/one woman. Commitment. Marriage.

It was bullshit, all of it. Daddy-walk-me-down-the-aisle crap. She knew better than to let it come back to haunt her.

Still, when she heard footsteps, she turned, almost jumped, expecting him. But it was Jay who came into the room and tried to appease her.

"Don't be angry with me," he said.

He'd gotten dressed, putting on board shorts and a tee shirt. The ultimate California boy. He'd been wearing similar clothes on the day she'd arrived.

"You were supposed to even the odds." But he'd rejected her in the name of brotherhood. In his own casual way, he was as much of a knight as Luke was.

"Even the odds? By being alone with you so you don't have to feel so connected to him? It wouldn't have worked. You would've been boffing me and thinking about him, the way you've been doing all along."

"It was only ever supposed to be a ménage."

"You know how the saying goes."

"That three's a crowd?"

He nodded. "He said he would kill me if I told you this, so if I end up dead, you'll know why."

"Tell me what?"

"That he—"

"No, don't!" Instant panic. Instant frenzy. She held up her hand, stopping him. "I already know what you're going to say."

"If you already know, then why does it matter if I say it?"

Because she didn't want to hear that Luke had admitted that he loved her. If the words were spoken, then she would have to decide if she loved him, too, and she wasn't in any condition to go that far. "Just keep his secret. Be his friend."

"I'm trying to be a friend to both of you."

"And you are." Probably the best friend either of them would ever have.

"If I know him, he's going to leave the house. And he won't come back until you're gone."

Sure enough, Jay knew his roommate. Luke didn't stick around. He left without saying good-bye, and Amber blew a painful sigh of relief. She was used to men abandoning her. It was what she expected. It made not loving him easier.

She finished packing, then booked a return flight to New Mexico. Although she could stay at her family's beachfront property in Malibu for the rest of her holiday, she wanted to get out of California as quickly as possible. Her discomfort, she supposed, at being in the same state as Luke.

"What time are you leaving?" Jay asked.

"Around two." She'd lucked out, getting a quick reservation. She'd arranged for a limousine to take her to the airport, too.

"I never made you the dinner you requested."

"Veal scaloppini? It's okay. I'll take one last breakfast, though."

"Sure. No problem." Jay shifted his bare feet. "He needed to get away for now, but he's going to freak out later."

She tried to downplay his remark. They were talking about Luke again. "He won't care that he missed breakfast."

"I was talking about the way he's going to feel when he comes back to an empty house."

"It won't be empty. You'll be here."

"I'm not what he's waited for his whole life."

"And neither am I." She forced a smile, trying to prove

who she was and who she would never be. "I'll be looking for a new ménage just as soon as the dust settles."

"Or the tattoo he gave you wears off?" Jay went into the kitchen to fix their meal.

Leaving her alone with a bumpy heart and the aching reminder of a red rose.

CHAPTER SEVENTEEN

I ventured down the hallway, wondering where Curtis was.
Should I start checking the rooms that branched off the corridor?

The music room? The study?

Yes, I thought. The study. Curtis knew that I loved to read
and that I would be familiar with its nooks and crannies.

I headed in that direction, and upon opening the door,
which creaked a bit, I inhaled the scent of leather bindings
and polished wood.

The walls were paneled in mahogany, and in front of the
fireplace were several well-cushioned chairs, a solid table and
a thick rug.

I proceeded to check the bookcases that formed a row of
aisles, searching for Curtis.

I found him, standing between two fiction-encompassed shelves and grinning devilishly. In his hands was an open book. He lifted it higher, allowing me to see the cover, which had a colorful illustration of a sea serpent on it.

My heart beat wildly from the want of him, but I raised my brows, prim as could be and played his silly game.

Was it fate or fortitude that had led him to a novel about serpents? Either way, I asked, "Is that the sort that eats virgins?"

"Yes, ma'am." He returned the book to its shelf. "And so am I."

Shamefully aroused, my knees wobbled beneath the folds of my skirt. Nonetheless, I continued the charade. "You shock me, sir."

"Do I?"

"You know you do."

He reached out and swept me into his arms. Up until then, we'd been speaking in hushed tones, but now we weren't speaking at all.

His lips sought mine, and we kissed passionately. He tasted wonderfully familiar and wantonly forbidden, reminding me of my favorite molasses toffee. When I was a child, I craved it, sneaking extra pieces out of the pantry when Cook wasn't looking.

We separated, and I said, "I want to pleasure you."

"You do pleasure me, my lady."

But I hadn't, at least not in the way I had in mind. I slid my hand to the front of his pants. "I want to do it with my mouth."

"Here?" *His voice crackled.* "Now?"

"I'll make your seed spill quickly." *Or I hoped that I would.* "That's possible, isn't it?" *I had no idea how long oral sex on a man might take.*

"I could climax just thinking about it."

I dropped to my knees, right there on the floor. But it wouldn't affect my appearance. My dress was already rumpled from the debauched picnic. "Then let me indulge you."

"What if your absence becomes apparent? Won't the duke wonder about your whereabouts if too much time has passed?"

"He'll be too busy socializing to watch the clock. Besides, he'll probably assume that I'm off with a group of ladies somewhere."

"What about Lady Milford? She might think that I'm avoiding her purposefully."

I considered my encounter with her. "She's too vain to think that."

Satisfied that Curtis wouldn't protest further, I unfastened his pants. "Will you coach me? I don't want to do it wrong."

"You won't."

But even so, he explained that I could use my hands along with my mouth, and he would move his hips to help create the motion. He warned me that his seed would be salty, and I prepared myself for the taste.

I was strangely aroused, reveling in the power that pleasuring him gave me. He grew instantly hard, and I stroked and sucked, making his breath rush from his lungs.

He kept his hands cupped under my chin. I sensed that he wanted to tunnel his fingers through my hair, but he was cautious about dislodging the portions of my coiffure that remained in place.

I took him as deeply as I could, and his cock teased my throat. He rocked back and forth in a copulating rhythm, just as he'd said he would.

Between the two of us, he wouldn't last. But that was our goal. I suspected that it was the most thrilling oral experience he'd ever had. Certainly the most illicit. He was struggling not to make aroused sounds.

Soon I felt the pressure of his release. His entire body tensed. He even lowered his hands to my shoulders to get a better grip on me.

His seminal fluid shot out, and I swallowed every salty drop. It made me thirsty for water, but I didn't flinch from the flavor. I even licked the head of his penis after the flow ended.

He stared down at me as if I were a bare-breasted siren emerging from the sea. His fantasy female.

I stood up and tucked him back into his pants. I fastened his fly, too.

As soon as I closed the last button, he kissed me, and the wetness of his mouth refreshed mine, lessening my thirst.

"You enchant me," he said, upon ending the kiss. "But it's more than that." He went somber, reaching for my hands and holding them. "So much more."

My heart twisted in my chest. "It's the same for me."

Once again, we'd acknowledged our love without professing it in the customary way. Behavior that had become a painful habit.

"You should go," he told me. "Return to the party."

"I need to repair my hair."

"I didn't muss it."

"From the rain." I met his gaze. "How long are you going to wait before you return?"

"Long enough to put distance between us."

Instead of remaining in the shadows, he walked me to the door, kissing me one last time.

While we were in the midst of it, that fateful door creaked open. We jumped apart, but it was too late.

We turned simultaneously and saw Lady Milford gaping at

us. Her shocked expression was proof that she didn't expect to find us together.

In my knee-weakening haze, I surmised that she'd come looking for Curtis with the assumption that he'd disappeared for so long because he wanted her to seek him out—to rendez-vous with her.

We were doomed, for I knew that she would never keep our secret. No amount of bribing or begging would do. She was a woman scorned.

Already she had vengeance in her eyes.

~

Two days after returning to Santa Fe, Amber rattled around in her mother's mansion, looking for something to do. The Spanish Colonial structure boasted the kind of beauty that only extreme wealth could buy.

As she walked into the ballroom, with its stained glass windows, glimmering green floor and carved wood accents, she was reminded of the first masquerade, where Luke had worn a red rose boutonniere on his lapel.

At the moment, her rose, the ever-fake tattoo, was covered by her blouse. It hadn't worn off yet and she hadn't taken an alcohol-swabbed cotton ball and rubbed it away. She'd con-sidered it, by God, but she hadn't summoned the courage to remove it.

The courage? Or the fear? She didn't know which, but once the tattoo was gone, she figured Luke was metaphorically gone, too.

She held up her arms, as if she were about to waltz across the floor with him. She even considered swaying to a nonexistent song, fantasizing about a man who hadn't even said good-bye.

Deep down, she hoped he would call, but he hadn't.

She, of course, would never call him. That would be too much like chasing after one of her runaway fathers.

"There you are," a familiar voice said.

Caught off guard, Amber dropped her waltz-poised arms and turned to look at her mother.

As always, Pia Pontiero was dressed to kill. As a fashion icon and beautifully aging blonde, her diva style was her signature.

Amber had inherited her mother's lean curves and lust for attention, but they were alike in other ways, too. Men had become insignificant to them, or so they liked to proclaim.

"I was just flitting about," Amber said.

"Yes, I saw." Mama sighed. "I'm worried about you."

"I'm fine."

"You're not yourself."

"Yes, I am." She was her child self, her teenage self. "But I'll snap out of it."

"Who is he, darling?"

The daughter feigned innocence. "He?"

"The man who's making you hurt?"

What was the point in lying? "Just someone from California. He attended the masque you hosted last summer."

"Then I know him?"

"No. He was there on behalf of a friend. I didn't introduce him to anyone."

"What's his name?"

"Luke." Before she was asked to expound, she added, "Turns out he's writing a screenplay about Curtis, and if he gets the movie made, he wants to play the part."

Pia widened her eyes. "*Our* Curtis?"

Amber nodded. "He's fascinated by Curtis's liaison with Lady Ellen."

"Is that why Luke pursued you? To get information about your ancestry?"

"No. But he did ask me to help him with his research."

"And did you?"

"I said that I would, but I didn't. I've never cared about Curtis the way you have."

"But I'll bet you do now."

Yes, Amber thought, for all the good it did.

"Did you know that Lady Ellen stayed in the Malachite Wing at the Duke of Auburn's estate? It had green floors."

Pia tapped her toe. "Like this." She added, "Curtis was in the Onyx Wing, which was down the hall. It's presumed that they snuck back and forth. But there's nothing left of the estate now."

Because it had been destroyed in World War Two, Amber thought, and hadn't been rebuilt.

"Curtis was killed just west of the garden," Pia added.

Amber glanced at the glass doors in the ballroom that led to a flagstone patio. Beyond that was the English-style garden attached to *this* mansion. "I wonder if flowers were scenting the air that day."

The older woman's voice went quiet. "Probably."

Feeling much too melancholy, Amber was reminded, once again, of the temporary rose on her body. "If you don't mind, I'm going to go for a walk."

"That's a good idea. Maybe it will help."

Or maybe it would make her lonelier. Either way, she was in the mood to reflect.

Not just about herself and Luke, but about Curtis and Lady Ellen, too.

❧

Mama and I waited in the tea parlor, seated in twin chairs and staring straight ahead. She clutched a fine linen handkerchief, and I clasped my hands on my lap.

Currently, the duke and Curtis were behind the closed doors of the duke's personal library, the room in which he conducted business.

During the party, Lady Milford had gone directly to the duke. She'd caused a deliberate spectacle, telling him, quite publicly, what she'd seen. Hence, the gathering had ended in scandal.

Regardless, the duke had behaved in a civil manner. He'd politely apologized to his guests, dismissing them from his home, whilst sending me and Mama to the tea parlor and requesting to speak with Curtis.

Thank goodness Papa hadn't been at the party. As usual he'd gone out for the day, preferring the company of his own friends. Soon, of course, he would hear about my indiscretion and call me a whore to my face.

Mama glanced over at me. Unlike Papa's predicted reaction, she gave me the benefit of the doubt.

"Was that the first time you kissed him?" she asked.

Should I lie? Should I claim that my relationship with Curtis was far more innocent than it was?

"No, Mama," I responded honestly. "I've kissed him many times before." Just that day I'd kissed the most intimate part of him. "He's my lover."

Her chest heaved with a weary breath. "The duke will probably use his power and prestige to have Mr. Wells banished from Glenmoor. I suspect that's what they're discussing. How soon he'll be leaving and the manner in which he'll be escorted to the next ship."

I thought about Sir Lancelot's exile. "I considered that this could happen."

"Considered it when?"

"On the first night I offered myself to him."

Mama frowned. "Do you love him?"

"Yes."

"Does he feel the same about you?"

"Yes, but we've never spoken the words."

She plucked at the embroidery on the hankie. "You could be mistaken that he loves you."

"The way you were mistaken about Papa? It isn't the same."

"You're certain then?"

"I've never been more certain of anything. Nor am I sorry about the risk I took to be with him. But I'm sorry about how this will affect you." The financial insecurity she would suffer. The shame of having a daughter who'd scandalized a well-respected duke.

"Oh, Ellen. I'm not worried for myself. It's your future, I fear."

"I'll get a job. I'll find a way to support myself. You and Papa, too." I had no skills or training to speak of, but surely

I could learn some sort of trade, earning enough to provide a modest dwelling and put food on the table.

"*I was talking about the future of your heart,*" she said.

I didn't respond, but I understood what she meant. She was worried that I would never love anyone as much as I loved Curtis, and she was right.

She leaned in close. "Maybe you should book passage on a ship, too. If Mr. Wells is banished, then maybe you should follow him to America."

My pulse scurried like a homeless cat. "You would encourage me to do that?"

"*I just did.*"

"*You should leave Papa and come with me.*"

She shook her head, letting me know that she intended to stay put. She cherished her wedding vows even if she no longer cherished Papa.

With mixed emotion, I put my cheek against her shoulder. "On what means would you survive, Mama?"

"*I would work, just as you said you would.*"

A job? At her age? All she'd ever known was being a countess. I didn't think the odds were in her favor.

Approaching footsteps caught our attention, and we turned in the direction of the sound.

The duke entered the room and stood formally in front of us. Curtis wasn't with him.

"I challenged Mr. Wells to a duel," he said flatly. "And he accepted."

The room went hazy, and I feared I might faint.

Mama reacted similarly, looking as unsteady as I felt. We'd never imagined that this would be the outcome of my affair.

Although duels weren't common in Glenmoor, the archaic practice wasn't forbidden, either. Normally duels were reserved for gentlemen, but the duke had once likened Curtis to a knight. I, too, thought of Curtis in that way.

The duke continued, "A pistol duel, where one shot is fired. Mr. Wells is going to complete the pistols I commissioned, as those will be the firearms used." The duke drilled me with his gaze. "As originally intended, your name will be engraved on them. That seems fitting, don't you think?"

So I would be literally and metaphorically responsible? So I would be injuring or fatally wounding one or possibly both of them? "Please don't do this."

"And what would you have me do? Banish Mr. Wells so you could run off after him, making an even bigger fool of me?"

I clutched the sides of my chair, and Mama blanched. Her support had been in vain.

The duke spoke to me again. "Mr. Wells will remain at the estate until the pistols are complete and the date of the duel is set." He sternly added, "As for you and your parents, I've arranged for you to stay in town, where you'll have absolutely no contact with Mr. Wells. You may, however, watch the duel if you're so inclined."

My dizziness worsened. "Why would Mr. Wells agree to this?" Why would Curtis willingly put himself in harm's way?

"Because he understands that I have a right to defend my honor." The duke's cold expression didn't change. "He also admitted that he loves you, and in his heart, you're worth dying for."

Dying for? I gripped my chair again.

"What if you're harmed, Your Grace?" I asked, attempting to sway him, to end his ludicrous plan.

"Me? That's highly unlikely. Mr. Wells is a fine shot. But I'm the better marksman."

I made another attempt to persuade him. "Even with a Western gun?"

"Yes."

"And Mr. Wells is aware of this?"

"Yes, he is." With that, the Duke of Auburn turned and walked away.

Confident in his victory.

CHAPTER EIGHTEEN

As Amber walked through the garden and passed a bentwood arbor, she approached a score of daisies blooming in pastel colors. The pink, light blue and yellow combination drew her closer, but it was a white flower, a traditional oxeye daisy, that she reached for.

He loves me. He loves me not.

She had no idea how that game got started, but it didn't apply to her, so she didn't pluck the petals.

According to Jay, Luke loved her.

Strange, but he didn't behave like a man in love, at least not in her mind. But what did she know about men in love?

With a sigh, she kept walking, taking the daisy with her.

When she came to a gazebo, one of her favorite spots in the garden, she plopped her butt down.

The hedge-flanked structure would be perfect for a wedding, she thought, suddenly frowning at her surroundings.

She glanced in the distance, where the rose garden flourished. No way was she going to head in that direction. The daisy was bad enough.

Lost in thought, she sat there clutching the flower. Then she glanced up and saw her mother coming toward her.

So much for privacy.

Pia had changed her clothes, but she was still fashionably groomed with Capri pants and gladiator-style sandals.

"I thought this was where I'd find you," the older woman said.

Apparently her favorite spot wasn't a secret. "It's a good place to think."

"Your young man is here, Amber."

Her world tilted. "Luke? He's here? At the mansion?"

Mama nodded. "Do you want to see him?"

Her grip on the stem of the flower got tighter. "Yes." But she feared her legs were too wobbly to carry her back to the house.

Luckily, Pia seemed aware. "I'll send him out here, okay?"

"Okay." Damn if she didn't feel like a silly little teenager. "What do you think of him?"

"He's handsome. And gentlemanly. I like him."

"Do you think he could play Curtis's part?"

Pia tilted her head. "Do you?"

"Yes."

"So do I. But I don't think he came here to discuss Curtis."

"I hope he makes this easy on me."

"Nothing is easy when it comes to men, darling."

Words to live by. Or watch a man die by, Amber thought. At least in Lady Ellen's case. As for herself, she shifted in her seat, as Pia returned to the mansion.

Amber wasn't wearing a watch, so she didn't know how many minutes had passed before she saw Luke. But he appeared like the modern-day knight she believed him to be. He was casually dressed, his thick dark hair slightly mussed and glinting in the sun. He looked natural in the setting.

He approached the gazebo, and she cautioned her heart to slow down, to stop beating so quickly, but the warning didn't work.

Instead of joining her on the bench, Luke stood on the lawn, and they stared at each other.

"I missed you," he said.

She battled nervousness. "Me, too."

Awkward silence, before he spoke again. "I thought roses were our flower."

Up until then, she'd forgotten that she was still holding

the daisy. Too late to dump it. Too late to act the femme fatale. "He loves me. He loves me not."

"You didn't remove any petals."

"I didn't play the game. I just wondered about it."

"Wondered what?"

"About its origin."

"It's French, *effeuiller la marguerite.*" He shrugged, seemingly shy. "Or something like that."

Although she'd holidayed many times in Paris, his romantic knowledge surpassed hers. "Did your sisters teach you that?"

He nodded. "My infamous siblings. I'd like for you to meet them."

She got insecure. "They'd probably hate me."

"Not if they knew that I loved you."

Oh, God. He'd said it. He'd admitted it to her. Because her hands started to shake, she put the daisy on her lap.

"This is where you're supposed to say it back," he said.

"I know. But I'm scared."

"Of saying it or feeling it?"

"Both." But she did feel it. And that was what scared her most of all. She patted the space next to her, inviting him to sit.

He moved forward, and when they were face-to-face, she looked into the darkness of his eyes.

"Are you still wearing the rose?" he asked.

She nodded. "Are you?"

He turned up his wrist to show her the floral-entwined sword.

She traced the temporary pattern. "Would you get one like that for real if I asked you to?"

He had a quick reply. "If you'd make yours real, too."

Permanent roses, permanent feelings. "What about our fight in L.A.? Aren't you worried that I'll need other men?"

"I was. But I'm not anymore. If you decide to be with me, I don't think there'll be any other men. I don't think you'd make a commitment without keeping it."

His trust should have baffled her, but it didn't. He was relying on her past—the marriage-minded girl behind the promiscuous woman.

"Now I'm really scared," she said.

He smiled and leaned in to kiss her, taking her response as encouragement.

And with good reason, she thought. When they separated, she was going to tell him that she loved him. Fear and all.

～

The day of the duel had arrived, and I was desperately afraid of losing the man I loved. Although I was permitted to watch, I was not allowed in the proximity.

So here I was in the bedchamber in which I'd once slept,

looking nervously out the window. At the moment there was nothing to see except the dark before dawn, but the duelers were scheduled to appear at first light.

I'd already been informed about the details. Neither man had chosen a second. Although there would be no stands-ins, the duke's private physician would be there, acting as witness. As for the pistols, each man would load his own and arrive at the location, ready for action. In that regard, it mirrored the American gunfights I'd read about, especially with the style of weapons being used.

Although the door to my suite had been locked from the outside, making me a temporary prisoner, I wasn't alone in my room. Mama was with me, and so was Miss Morgan, my former lady's maid. She, too, peered out the window. Mama, however, refused to wait and watch. She said that she couldn't bear it.

Neither could I, but I needed to support Curtis, to make a connection with him, even from afar.

I turned to Miss Morgan, recalling her affection for the stableboy and said, "If you love Billy, you should tell him how you feel."

"Does Mr. Wells know how you feel?" she asked.

"Yes, but I never said the words to him, and he never said them to me."

"Do the words matter so much?"

I studied her appearance, her fragile complexion and curly red hair, twisted into a bun. "I think they do."

"I heard that Mr. Wells told the duke that he loves you." She made a perplexed face. "This seems so extreme for the duke. The duel, I mean. I always thought the duke to be a more forgiving man."

"I never expected anything like this, either." If I'd known that I'd be putting Curtis's life in danger, I wouldn't have gone to his room that first night.

"Maybe they intend to misfire," she said. "Maybe they secretly agreed upon it."

My pulse beat within my body. Was that possible? Dumb shooting wasn't permissible under the code, but who would be the wiser?

Mama spoke her opinion. "It seems likely, Ellen. Truly, it does. That practice used to happen all the time."

I turned to face her. "I think it's likely, too." The one-shot condition of the duel would be fulfilled, and both men would walk away unharmed with their honor intact, as long as their ruse went undiscovered.

Mama sent me a gentle smile, and hope filled our hearts.

Time pressed on, and as the sun peeked through the sky, the men appeared on the lawn. The physician stood off by himself. Curtis and the duke wore dark clothes, blending into the murky dawn. But I knew who was who.

My hopeful heart thudded against my chest. I could even hear it beating in my ears.

As I watched the scene unfold, the duelers stood back to back with their loaded weapons in hand. It all seemed so very real. But that was the point, wasn't it?

As they began to walk the number of agreed-upon paces, Miss Morgan reached for my hand.

"It will be all right," she said. "It will."

But she was wrong. They turned and fired, and Curtis stumbled and fell backwards, hitting the ground.

I screamed and released Miss Morgan's hand, determined to rush to him. I tugged on the locked door, but it was to no avail. Mama came up behind me, cradling me within her arms.

She cooed, hushing me. Curtis might only have suffered an injury, she said, and would recover to live another day.

But she, too, was wrong.

The doctor checked his vitals and pronounced him dead at the scene, for he'd taken a bullet straight to the heart. Within no time, his blood-soaked body was covered in a cloth and placed on a small boat, captained by a lone fisherman.

From there, his burial was swift and impersonal. I soon learned that he'd been tossed into the sea, far enough that he wouldn't wash back upon the shore and with the merest of prayer.

Curtis was truly gone, and I'd been denied the right to see

*him, unable to lay my hand upon his cheek and tell him, even
in death, that I loved him.*

~

"I love you," Amber said, making Luke lose his breath. He'd
clung to the hope that she shared his feelings, but hearing her
say it made all the difference.

He touched her cheek. "I love you, too."

"Jay was right."

"Yeah he was."

She smiled. "Damn him anyway."

In spite of her humor, she still looked scared, but Luke figured it was a good kind of scared. He knew that feeling, too.

"Do you want to walk through the rose garden?" she
asked.

"That sounds perfect." He stood up, and she put the daisy
on the bench, where she left it.

Once they were surrounded by "their" flower, many of
them red, he looked around, impressed with what he saw.

"Those are old garden roses," he told her. "The type that
were cultivated before eighteen sixty-seven. That's the year
the first hybrid tea was introduced." He gestured to another
group of flowers. "And those are modern garden roses, introduced after eighteen sixty-seven."

"I had no idea that you were such an authority."

"Did you think I was giving you roses without any knowledge of how they were grown?"

She looked at him with wonder. "Other men would have."

"I'm not other men." He kissed her, softly, slowly, letting the feeling between them linger.

Afterward, she sighed, sounding sweet, girlish, and less afraid. Nothing could have pleased him more.

She spoke, switching gears, and drawing him into the past. "Mama said that Curtis was shot near the garden on the duke's estate."

Intrigued, Luke angled his head. "What else did she tell you?"

"That Lady Ellen stayed in the Malachite Wing, and Curtis had a suite in the Onyx Wing." Amber took his hand. "We have a gun he designed. Come on, I'll show you."

She led him into the mansion, where they entered a sitting room with mosaic floors and Southwestern art. Positioned in a corner was a tall glass-shelved case.

She retrieved a beautifully crafted six-shooter, opened the cylinder and rotated it, showing him that the chambers were empty. Then she gave him the gun.

It felt wonderfully strange to hold a piece of Curtis Wells in his hand. "Where did this come from?"

"It was passed down from my great-grandmother."

"From Sophie?" Curtis's daughter? The child he barely knew? "How did she end up with it?"

"It was left behind when Curtis walked away from her and her mother."

"Did you know Sophie?"

"No. But before she died, she supposedly babbled on about how Curtis had come back from the dead to see her. But she was old and senile. She didn't know what she was talking about."

"Maybe she saw his ghost before she died." Luke shifted the revolver in his hand. "Maybe that was his way of reaching out to her."

"And maybe she was just a crazy old soul, haunted by his legacy." Amber frowned. "Did you know that the pistols used in the duel were tossed into the ocean with Curtis's body? That gave me the creeps when I was a kid, and now it just makes me sad."

"I wonder what Curtis's life would have been like if he'd been the one to survive, if he could've stayed with Lady Ellen." Luke returned the gun. "I wish I could change the ending of their story."

"And give them what they lost?" She placed the antique pistol back on the shelf. "I wish you could, too. But it wouldn't be accurate."

No, he thought. But it was a nice dream.

My nightmare continued, but I was too numb to care.

Soon after Curtis's death, the duke offered Papa a new deal, sealing my final fate. They arranged for me to leave Glenmoor for good, to never be seen or heard from again.

For my exile, the duke had agreed to provide a seaside cottage for my parents, with monthly allotments to Papa and an allowance for Mama.

She was distraught over my departure, but she understood my plight. I'd become no better than a leper in Glenmoor. Papa and the duke had seen to it.

Today I arrived at my new residence, a convent on an island off the coast of Italy. It had been the duke's idea that I live among sequestered nuns, and his decision, cold as it was, gave Mama a small measure of comfort, considering her affinity with Catholicism. Papa had no opinion. He'd already disowned me.

Mama accompanied me on the journey, and so did the duke. He wanted to ensure my fate, to handle it personally. But that was his nature.

Not once during the voyage did I glance his way or speak to him. My infidelity was wrong, but what he'd done was far worse. He'd baited Curtis to his death, preying on my beloved's honor.

Once the three of us were inside the convent, Mama got tearful and clung to my hand. I held on to her, too, but a hollow ache kept me from crying.

Sister Maria, an older woman with craggy features and a gentle voice, led us to my room. I was expecting it to be modest and tidy.

But as the nun opened the door, I saw a miracle before my eyes.

There stood Curtis.

Gloriously handsome. Alive and well.

Sister Maria smiled and left the room, Mama gasped in shock, and I began to quake.

"My lady," Curtis said to me in his untamed drawl.

Still quaking, I rushed straight into his arms and cried upon his broad shoulder, my emotions flooding to the surface.

Finally, when I lifted my face to his, he dried my tears and gave me a chaste kiss, rife with the wonder of being together.

As I turned in his arms and looked at the duke, my heart softened for my former betrothed. He was indeed a good and honorable man. I thanked him in a soft voice, and he nodded and smiled, pleased with my affection.

Curtis released his gentle hold on me and suggested that Mama step outside of the room with him, giving the duke and me a moment to talk.

Before Curtis escorted Mama into the hallway, he glanced back at me, and our gazes met and held, befitting our hearts.

Mama took his arm, and they quietly departed. I assumed that Curtis was going to provide Mama with details of what had transpired between himself and the duke, just as the duke would explain it to me.

Once we were alone, the duke said, "I was angry at first. So angry that I told Mr. Wells that I should challenge him to a duel, and it was his reaction that gave me pause."

"Is that when he told you that he loved me?"

"Yes. When he expressed that he would gladly die for you, I realized then that he loved you in the way I'd loved my wife. In a way I myself could never love you. It seemed wrong to deny you what he could give you."

My eyes misted. "So you suggested a mock duel to fool society and save your reputation?"

"Otherwise, I feared that I would appear weak. Especially if he left the country and you followed him."

"Mama suggested that I go with him, but she refused to go with me."

"I suspected that would be the case," he responded. "She is also a factor in why I devised the ruse. I was concerned for her well-being."

So he'd struck this new bargain with my father as a means

to provide for my mother. I thanked him once again for everything he'd done.

We both went silent for a moment, then I asked, "How many other people were involved? How many knew the truth?"

"Aside from Mr. Wells and me? The doctor and the boat captain. The doctor is a trusted friend, and the captain is a devout man who made the arrangements with the convent."

I struggled to fit all of the pieces together, to lock them into place. "What about the duel itself? Why did you use the six-shooters? And how did Curtis—Mr. Wells," I corrected, respecting the duke's formality, "how did he bleed that way?"

"We needed time to develop our plan, so having Mr. Wells complete the pistols provided extra time. As for the blood, it was staged. A theatre prop beneath his jacket."

"Were the bullets blanks?"

"Yes. The only truth to the story is that the pistols were discarded while Mr. Wells was on the boat. He, himself, flung them overboard."

In my mind's eye, I saw them floating to the bottom of the ocean like a sunken treasure, with sea creatures, real and mythical, swimming around them.

"Why didn't you tell me all of this ahead of time?"

"I thought it best for your grief to appear genuine, and Mr. Wells abided by my wishes. His gratitude holds no bounds."

"Nor does mine. I wish there was something I could do to repay you."

"Just be well, my lady."

"I will. Always."

I moved forward to embrace him, and afterward he said, "I'll find another young woman to marry. I still intend to produce an heir."

I smiled. It pleased me to think of him with a wife and child. "As well you should."

Our conversation ended on a high note, and he reentered the hallway to join Mama, calling Curtis back to my side.

We stood in the tiny room, with its narrow bed, petite side table, and wooden cross nailed to the wall. For me, it was the most magical place I'd ever been.

I sought his gaze, and he sought mine.

Finally I spoke the words out loud. "I love you."

Curtis caressed my cheek. "I love you, too. From now on, we'll never be apart."

Never, ever, I thought, entranced by his touch.

"I have some money," he told me. "Cash that I brought to Glenmoor. Not enough to last forever, but enough to give us a good start. And I can always rebuild my success with a new name."

I understood that we would have to live under assumed names. "I don't care who we are, as long as we're together." To *me, it didn't matter that Curtis Wells and Lady Ellen would be no longer.*

"We'll travel through Europe and the Orient. America, too. Someday we'll visit Sophie and tell her our story. But not until she's old enough to understand and keep her daddy's secret."

"She'll probably think it's marvelously romantic."

"I hope so. I want her to be proud of me."

I was proud of him. He was my heaven and earth, and no matter what we did or where we went, I was certain that we would be happy.

～

Amber and Luke spent several days in Santa Fe, then returned to California. Although Amber would remain connected to her privileged lifestyle, she had agreed to live with Luke, to become part of his world, too.

As they approached the front door, he said, "I'm going to call the landlord about the option to buy this place. I want to establish roots."

She smiled. "That's a great idea. This house fits you." The Hollywood Hills location, she thought, the art deco décor.

"I want it to fit us, Amber."

"It does. I like it here."

"Good." His gaze locked gently onto hers. "Because you're going to marry me someday."

Her heartbeat accelerated. Was that a proposal? A wish? A hope? A peek into the future? "Someday?"

"When you're ready. When we can take the time to plan it right."

A light breeze stirred the air between them, and in the background she could hear sounds from the city. "The wedding I always dreamed about?"

"Except the father of the bride part. I'm sorry I can't fix that for you."

"It's okay," she said. "I can focus on new details. A new dress. New everything."

Luke pulled her close. "Whatever you decide is fine."

She melted against him. "I can't believe I'm even thinking about getting married."

"I'm just planting the seed," he responded.

And watching it grow, she thought.

They went inside, where Jay waited to greet them. But he was expecting their arrival. Luke had called ahead.

"Well, look who's here," Jay said, flashing a casual grin.

Amber stepped forward to hug him, and he rocked her in a sideways motion. She could tell how happy he was for her and Luke. He was, without a doubt, their dearest friend.

They separated, and Luke spoke to his roommate. "She just agreed to marry me."

"Someday," Amber added, with girlish exhilaration.

"Someday soon, I'll bet," Jay remarked, bringing everyone to a sweet hush. Then he said, "I have to work today. But I'll see you guys tonight, okay? I'll fix a nice meal, and you can tell me all about your gooey, lovey stuff over dinner."

Amber smiled. She suspected that he was going to make veal scaloppini.

He turned to leave, and she realized that he could easily be the man who walked her down the aisle, who gave her away to the groom.

It wasn't the threesome she'd originally intended, but somehow it worked—the mock-wedding trio participating in a real wedding, with heartfelt feelings between them.

She watched Jay shoot Luke a brotherly nod on his way out the door.

"He's a good guy," she said to Luke.

"Yeah, he is. He's still hooked on Beverly, though. Nothing has changed in that regard. I wonder if we can convince him to see her."

"We already tried that."

"I know, but we can keep trying."

"And drive him crazy with it?"

"Why not? He drove us nuts about how we felt about each other."

"So he did." She latched onto Luke, nuzzling against the warmth of his body.

"You know what else I think we should do?" he asked, then answered the question himself. "We should repair Curtis and Lady Ellen's lives."

"Are you asking for my permission to alter the facts in your screenplay? To change history?"

"I guess I am. It's your family. Your ancestry. I don't want to do anything that wouldn't sit well with you."

"Then go ahead," she told him, unable to refuse. "Use your creative license." She had no doubt that he would come up with a clever way to give Curtis and Lady Ellen a happy ending. But somehow, it seemed like the right thing to do, as if a new version would make it real. "I'm sure Sophie would be pleased."

"In my story, she isn't going to be a crazy old lady. She'll be a young woman who gets a surprise visit from her father, a man who'd supposedly died when she was a child."

"It sounds wonderful already. Just like you."

"I'm glad you think so."

Luke leaned in for a kiss that went from soft to sweet to sizzling, all within the blink of a storyteller's eye.

He took her hand, leading her to the room they would now share. He closed the door, and they stripped off their clothes and climbed into bed.

One man. One woman.

"Kneel over me," he told her.

"Over you where?" she asked.

"Here." He maneuvered her right where he wanted her—straddling his face, backward, so she could see how aroused he was.

She would have swayed had she been on her feet. She loved looking at him: the ripple of muscle on his stomach, the masculine shape of his navel, the aggressive rise of his cock.

He kissed her clit, and she rubbed against his mouth. Offering him more, she opened herself up. He accepted the invitation and slipped his tongue inside.

"You're mine," he said, between naughty licks. "All mine."

Talk about teasing his future bride. She got wetter than wet.

Taking their foreplay to the next level, she lowered her head, and they went sixty-nine. He continued lapping at her juices, and she did everything she could to please him, swirling around the head of his penis, sucking the length of his shaft, cupping his testes.

Together, they made oral magic, and she came all over him. He didn't come, but he was leaking like crazy. He pulled back and caught his breath.

She smiled her satisfaction. He grabbed a condom out of his handy-dandy nightstand drawer and made good use of it. Before Amber could consider their next position, he had her flat on her back.

He pushed inside, turning her post-orgasmic state into a wonderfully tortured ache. She could actually feel how much he loved her.

But the feeling was mutual.

She clawed the bed while he moved. He was it. All she wanted. All she needed. Her girlhood dreams had gone beyond fantasy and into the realm of a reality she'd never expected. This man, this gorgeous warrior, this rose-bearing knight, was going to be her husband. Every day for the rest of her life, he would be there.

To kiss her, to ravish her, to treat her with tenderness and care. Whatever she desired, he was the one.

Sir Luke and Lady Amber, making history of their own.